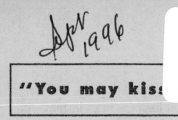

"You may kiss

Toria snapped to attention.

Had she just now promised to love, honor and cherish this man for richer, for poorer?

Last night, in the safety of her home, Toria had been too occupied with practical matters—laying out guest towels for her new husband and his daughter and vacuuming with a zeal she never knew she possessed—to think about her sacred and speedy vows to Nick.

She looked at the judge, who stared implacably at the clock hanging on the wall over the door. She looked at little Anya solemnly holding a bouquet. She looked down at her own left hand now adorned with a band of gold. She forced herself to look up at Nick. As her eyes met his, she suddenly wanted to run.

But she was a woman of her word. And wouldn't back out on a deal. Or a kiss from Nick.

Dear Reader,

Sometimes becoming a family takes years. But for three unlikely couples, it happens in an instant—in the new SUDDENLY...A FAMILY miniseries!

As any single parent can tell you, courtship with kids is anything but slow and easy. But three popular American Romance authors show you how much fun it can be to be caught in a "family affair."

Join Vivian Leiber at the green-card wedding of a single father and the woman who rushes to his aid and lingers in his heart. Vivian wrote this story as a special love letter to the town of Naperville, Illinois, where she grew up.

Be sure to look for all the upcoming titles in the SUDDENLY...A FAMILY miniseries!

Regards,

Debra Matteucci
Senior Editor & Editorial Coordinator
Harlequin Books
300 East 42nd Street
New York, NY 10017

Vivian Leiber

MARRYING NICKY

Harlequin Books

TORONTO • NEW YORK • LONDON
AMSTERDAM • PARIS • SYDNEY • HAMBURG
STOCKHOLM • ATHENS • TOKYO • MILAN
MADRID • WARSAW • BUDAPEST • AUCKLAND

To Eastman and Joseph

ISBN 0-373-16655-9

MARRYING NICKY

Chapter One

Nicholas Sankovitch looked up at the Northeastern spire of Old Main, bejeweled with windows that sparkled in the late-afternoon pause before sunset.

She was there. At the tower's very peak, like a princess in a fairy tale.

But he was no knight, no prince, Nick thought as he hoisted the moving box onto his broad shoulder. And he would never see her again. Though he would sell his very soul to have her come, just once, to the window as he passed this last time.

"You never had a chance," he muttered under his breath.

His memory of her, as precious as gold to Nick, would have to sustain him for the rest of his life. Her sherry-colored eyes, thick dark chestnut hair, longer and more luxuriant than current fashion, rosebud lips—sometimes touched with lipstick, sometimes not—were burned into his mind. He would forever remember her prim and proper clothes that only suggested, but how he ached at the mere suggestion. And the scent of roses—*her* scent—subtle but unforgettable, that had embraced him as he passed her in a hall or on the campus walkways, would always follow Nick.

He had never spoken to her, sensing that such a woman wouldn't care for him—a scientist, yes, a respected one, of course, but, still, at heart, a rough-hewn peasant.

He would carry her image forever, an image made bittersweet by the knowledge that she was never, would never be, within reach.

"You never had a chance," he said again, and carried his burden across the empty campus.

A FADED PINK-AND-GOLD ribbon adorned her tiny waist and a corsage of violets was stuck to her shoulder. The strong, confident arms of a British cavalry officer—his porcelain sword chipped ever so slightly at the tip—guided her around the eight-inch dance floor. The music was like wind chimes, "The Black Forest Waltz." Captured by a hand-crafter on the brink of speaking to each other, they looked as if their words of love had remained unspoken for a hundred years.

Professor Victoria Tryon looked up from exam number sixteen. *Only thirty-six more to go,* she thought.

Rewarding her diligence at grading midterms one through fifteen, she let her eyes linger on the music box. It was a familiar, no-cost, lo-cal indulgence. Whatever country, whatever time, whatever world the music-box dancers inhabited, Toria often let herself go there. If only for a moment's visit.

I have . . . almost everything a woman could want, she mused as she focused on the cavalry officer—so gentlemanly, so chivalrous, so tender in his embrace.

Pop!

So much for fantasy.

"Anya, don't snap your bubble gum," Toria said with mock sternness. "It's not very ladylike."

The eight-year-old seated on a tweed footstool in front of the music box solemnly swallowed her gum.

"And you shouldn't swallow it," Toria added. "It stays in your stomach for seven years, and sometimes, if you've swallowed too much of the stuff, your stomach will explode when you least expect it."

Anya's sable brown eyes widened with horror, and Toria remembered that she shouldn't joke with Anya. American kids were sophisticated enough to know that gum was digested like everything else and jaded enough to ignore adult scare tactics.

"Sorry, it's just an old wives' tale," Toria explained. "Your stomach won't really explode. But you still shouldn't do it. Throw it in the wastebasket next time."

Anya stared at Toria until she was satisfied she wasn't being lulled into a false sense of security about the possibility of her stomach exploding. Then she smiled—freckles brightening, eyes impish and one tooth jauntily loose. And Toria remembered every reason why she loved the little girl.

As Anya carefully wound up the music box once more, Toria returned to exam sixteen. Rereading the first sentence, she wondered how North Central's star quarterback could have reached the age of eighteen with such dismal writing skills.

Her mission was to change all that, of course. For him and fifty-one other freshmen. And in just one semester, too, she thought.

The bell at the top of Old Main tolled loudly. Toria's teacup rattled, a pencil rolled off her desk, and she wondered whether the building would collapse. Professors and students had been wondering the same thing since Old Main had been built in 1870.

The bell sounded for the second time.

Toria closed her eyes in frustration at the mangled English on the page before her.

The third.

Wait a minute! She looked up at Anya, studying her closely.

Fourth.

Something was not right.

And finally a fifth.

Anya, the daughter of Professor Nicholas Sankovitch of the environmental sciences department, visited Toria often in the afternoons when Naperville's elementary school let out. But she always obeyed her father's five o'clock curfew. And although Toria had never actually met Anya's father, she knew that he kept close tabs on his only child.

Professor Sankovitch had a reputation for being intensely private, though coeds were known to openly appraise his physical endowments. Toria herself would never do that sort of thing.

Besides, though she had glimpsed him at faculty get-togethers, she had never approached him. Perhaps she feared he would express disapproval of Anya's visits. Or perhaps there was something so intensely masculine about him that he embodied a reproach to her austere but utterly feminine life.

"Anya, it's already five o'clock," Toria said. "The afternoon flies when you're here."

Toria's office was at the peak of one of the spires of Old Main, and few students—fewer faculty—braved the four flights of narrow stairs to see her.

Toria had more than once caught herself listening for Anya's quick, delicate steps so full of childish exuberance.

But today...

One of Anya's purple hair ribbons was missing from her unkempt pigtails. Her face was splattered with watercolor—from art class, no doubt—and Toria had been presented with the artistic effort, which, still damp, hung on the back of her door. Anya's dress was missing three decorative buttons and was covered with paint, grime and the remains of what looked to be a spaghetti lunch. Anya's socks didn't match, and she had three *Beauty and the Beast* bandages stuck on her right knee.

In other words, nothing was out of place for Anya.

But a single tear slid down Anya's cheek just before the little girl brutally wiped it away.

"What's wrong?" Toria asked, sitting beside her on the floor.

The music stopped. Anya looked away, out the window at the setting sun, which was just disappearing behind the stark branches of oak and maple. Holding something in, something terrible.

When Anya turned back to Toria, her eyes glittered with tears and her cheeks were flushed bright red.

"What is it?" Toria drew Anya into her arms.

Anya buried her head in Toria's soft gray cotton cardigan. Toria put her arms around Anya and soothingly rubbed her back.

Anya mumbled something.

"What?"

"I said it's a secret."

"Well, then, you don't have to tell me."

Anya sat up straight.

"Oh, but I want to."

"All right, then tell me."

"My father says I can't."

Toria felt her heart go thaddump! as a half dozen horrifying scenarios tripped through her mind. She felt conflicted. If it was important enough to make Anya cry, perhaps it was important enough that Toria should know. On the other hand, Toria shouldn't get involved in a family matter. Should she...?

"I'll tell you, anyhow," Anya said in a rush. "We're moving."

"Oh." Toria very nearly added, Is that all? then remembered that for Anya, moving away might be very traumatic. After all, she and her father had come to this country from Byleukrainia—that tiny, struggling former Soviet Republic—only the spring before. Moving to America must have been very hard on Anya.

Still, it seemed odd that the Sankovitches would move from North Central College so soon. The school had been delighted when Professor Sankovitch had received a huge private foundation grant to pursue his studies of the ecosystem of the surrounding prairie land. Why would he make a move now? Toria wondered. Had another college made him a better offer...?

"When are you leaving?" Toria asked neutrally.

"Tonight," Anya said and burst into tears again.

Toria held the girl for several minutes, Anya's body shaking with racking sobs.

Toria's heart throbbed in her throat. She nearly felt like crying herself, yet her training as an academic made her stop and consider the possibilities.

There had to be some sort of mistake. Academics didn't just pack up and move in the middle of the night. Gossip traveled between schools well in advance of the many scheduled visits and interminable guest lectures that, after much handwringing on the part of a school's appointments committee, resulted in an offer. If Professor Sankovitch was moving to another school, everyone at North Central College— even Toria, in a different department, in her isolated spire of Old Main—would have heard about it weeks ago.

Besides, he had this grant that allowed him millions of dollars to continue his research. No scientist in his right mind would abandon that work.

"Are you absolutely sure?" Toria asked as soon as the girl had composed herself. Anya's remaining hair ribbon had slipped from its place. Absently Toria pulled off the elastic bands and began braiding Anya's hair. She retied the ribbon.

Anya nodded solemnly. "Tonight," she said. "We're leaving tonight. I'll miss you so much. Today is the last day I'll ever see you."

Toria suddenly had a thought.

"Are you going back to Byleukrainia?" she asked. "Perhaps your father's taking you back for a visit..."

Although why anyone would take a chance, given the country's constant upheaval, Toria couldn't fathom.

"No!" Anya said emphatically. "We're moving so we won't ever have to go back there again."

"Oh. Where are you going to move to?"

"I don't know. But Daddy won't be able to work as a professor anymore. He might become a cab driver."

Toria hid her surprise and suppressed her curiosity. What Anya needed was comfort, not questions. She put her arms around the girl and consoled her as she cried for a little while longer.

Outside, the college's gas lamps—wired for electricity just after World War I—flickered on and shone their light on the sparkling, damp carpet of red, yellow and ruddy brown leaves of the quad. The late-afternoon clumps of students had scattered. One couple sat holding hands on the steps of the science building. A crisp breeze carried the smell of burning leaves into the office, and Toria heard the distant bellowing of the first evening train at the Naperville station.

Anya had quieted in the folds of her arms, and Toria wondered if it was possible that she had fallen asleep.

"'Fessor Toria, can I hear the music box one more time?" Anya asked quietly, pulling away from her.

"Sure," Toria said absently, still puzzled by the Sankovitches' impending departure. She even considered calling her friend Missy, also in the English department. Missy knew everything about everyone's business—but making that phone call would mean revealing Anya's secret.

She wound up the music-box key and the two sat watching the tiny dancers. Usually, the sight, the soothing music would calm Toria, remind her of a different time and place. A time of chivalry and honor. A place of romance and devotion.

But tonight, the familiar music and the familiar turn of the dancers gave her no comfort.

"I wish he wasn't making us move again," Anya said dismally. "He's being such a meanie."

Meanie?

That did it!

Ordinarily slow—make that snail slow—to anger, slower still to involve herself in what she regarded as others' private matters, Toria looked at the girl and felt the whisper-soft voice of fate.

Not if I have anything to say about it, Toria silently vowed.

Chapter Two

This was definitely going to make her a little late for her date with Lean Cuisine.

By the time Toria had calmed Anya, packed her own briefcase with exams sixteen through fifty-two and stopped with Anya at the faculty mailboxes on the first floor of Old Main, it was dark outside. Too dark to merely wave goodbye to Anya, Toria reasoned, as she stood outside the environmental sciences department.

Anya slipped her hand into Toria's as they walked together to Professor Sankovitch's office.

I'm just going to introduce myself, Toria cautioned inwardly. *And explain why Anya was late.*

And maybe just ask what the heck was going on.

Toria could see it now—it would be so straightforward. Professor Sankovitch would say something that would clear up this matter of moving, Toria would feel like an idiot for asking and then she'd go home.

There had to be a logical explanation, of course. Something simple and uncomplicated.

But then they stepped into his cramped office.

Cardboard boxes—some half packed, others taped and stacked by the door—were everywhere. The steel desk drawers had been pulled out and six of the seven were empty.

Professor Sankovitch had his back to the door, his concentration focused on the contents of the top drawer of a file cabinet behind his desk. Even from behind, Toria could see he was tall and broad, his blue-black hair a sharp contrast to his sun-touched skin. He wore a deep spruce-colored flannel shirt and jeans so faded from wear that Toria could feel their softness even from across the room. And she could see the hardness of his legs and buttocks.

"Hunk," Missy Schroeder had written on a note passed discreetly during a grueling faculty meeting.

Definite hunk material. Too bad he won't give me the chance to do further research.

Toria had professed to be appalled, although she didn't specify whether that feeling was directed at passing notes during speeches by the chairman of the department or at making untoward evaluations of colleagues.

Missy didn't care about either.

If it was true he was moving, many people would be taken by surprise. Missy would be devastated.

"Daddy!" Anya cried out, breaking from Toria's hold and flinging herself into Sankovitch's arms. He turned just in time to catch his daughter, and his sapphire eyes crinkled with delight.

When he saw Toria, those eyes narrowed and his sharp, Slavic jaw clenched tightly. His cheekbones were broad and high, hinting at his western Russian heritage. His nose was long and broad, flattened at one side with a thin scar running to his eye. The scar whitened as he flushed. He stared at her warily.

Hunk?

Definitely.

His pose could be duplicated in the very finest beefcake calendars—not that Toria would be caught dead buying one. Maybe just peeking at the sales counter.

But Toria's concern for Anya made her square her shoulders—no quivering awe for her. She jutted out her chin and extended her hand to firmly shake his.

Toria knew that when she was on the warpath, she might have been only five-three, but she was invincible.

"Hello, I'm Victoria Tryon," she said crisply. "Please call me Toria. I'm in the English department. My office is at the top of Old Main. Anya's been visiting me sometimes."

Feeling as if she was babbling under his flat, emotionless gaze and also noticing that he had made no move to shake her outstretched hand, she gestured at Anya.

Professor Sankovitch's face softened only slightly. Still wary, he took her hand and shook it firmly and solemnly. The handshake was perfectly businesslike, and yet there was something sexual in his touch, but she couldn't have described exactly what it was.

"Hunk," Missy had written in her loopy scrawl.

Toria bit her lip and cautioned herself that she would not, under any circumstances, relate this experience to Missy.

"Toria," she said. "Call me Toria."

"All right. Tor-ee-a," he replied, savoring each syllable of her name, drawing out every nuance so that the word sounded less like the shortened name of the beloved monarch of the repressed British Empire and more like that of a sex kitten.

Missy would have loved to hear him say her name out loud, Toria thought.

"Please, call me Nick," he said lazily.

And he waited. But she didn't. She wouldn't.

"My daughter has said a lot about you," he continued. "All good. She has made a pest of herself often, I understand."

"Anya's been a delight. I always look forward to seeing her."

His eyes met hers. Those eyes, so blue, so crystalline blue—the blue of cool sapphires and a clear summer sky. The smile broad, seemingly open. The English, spoken tentatively, piquantly accented, meant to suggest friendliness, openness. Come here, trust me, come here.

Toria looked away.

"Daddy, I told her," Anya said, pulling from his embrace. "I'm sorry. I didn't tell anybody else. I promise."

At his forehead, a single trace of blue vein throbbed. Toria nearly reached out to him as she had to his daughter. But when he looked at her, he was in control again.

"Professor. Toria. This is a family matter. I'm sure you understand."

There was no request for sympathy or understanding. Through heavily lidded eyes he appraised every inch of her body with a burnished regard.

Toria felt a blush come at his look—starting at the roots of her hair and going all the way down to her toes.

The appraisal had an offhand masculine arrogance—clearly he was a man who had never understood the reason to separate sex from any other part of his life.

Still, the appraisal wasn't strictly sexual.

Trust, Toria intuited. Trust.

He turned his head, still looking at her from under coal black lashes and made his evaluation of Toria.

"I know I don't have any right to be, but still, I'm concerned about your daughter," Toria pressed. "She seems very unhappy with this move. And it's so sudden."

His eyes flashed with surprise. He reached into the front pocket of his work shirt.

"Anya, you must be starved," he said, looking past Toria as if she weren't even there. "Here's some change. Run down to the vending machine and get yourself a snack. Remember, no candy before dinner. Pick one of the granola bars or the pretzels."

Anya didn't need prompting, and within seconds, her footsteps receded down the hallway to the faculty lounge. Finding a place to sit, Nick dumped a stack of papers from his desk chair and stretched his long, lean legs to rest his feet on the desk.

"Families move. It happens," he said, as if language were a barrier to further explanation.

She felt a surge of indignation on behalf of Anya. After all, she had spent the past hour comforting the girl.

And she knew his English was as good as anyone else's at the college. Even in the short weeks of the semester, he had already developed a reputation for intense, provocative lectures.

She was being played for a fool and she knew it and didn't like it. Not one little bit.

"Your daughter is very upset," she pointed out.

"My daughter is my business," he said, his inflection clear and daunting.

Toria took a deep breath.

He was absolutely right, of course. She had stepped over the line by challenging him, and ordinarily she would have apologized immediately and backed off. She wouldn't want a total stranger interfering with her own child rearing—assuming, of course, she ever had children.

But the memory of her little friend's tears—or maybe the vision of her office, empty and forlorn—kept her from retreating completely.

"Where are you planning on going?" she asked, mimicking the pleasantness her mother had often employed in sticky social situations.

She felt like a hypocrite with a bright, mindless smile on her face, but she wanted to know.

"Anywhere nearby?" she added brightly, having just perched on the smaller file cabinet by the door, on top of a few midterm-examination blue books.

"We don't know," he said slowly, spreading his broad hands wide.

"You don't even know where you're going?"

So much for Mom's perkiness—just plain old honest disbelief would do the trick.

He looked away, seeming to study a half-empty bookshelf. A travel clock on his desk ponderously ticked. From several doors down, lab monkeys were rattling their cages. The computer lab hummed.

"I like Anya very much," Toria said, breaking the uncomfortable silence. "I hope everything's all right. She's a very special girl. This summer, when I was preparing for classes, we'd get an ice cream from the Good Humor man. And now, after school, she shows me all her artwork and tells me about her day. We do her homework together sometimes. I like her, probably too much. But there it is. I worry about her, and if there was anything that I could do to help, I'd want you to tell me."

He sighed and put his feet on the floor. Elbows on the desk, he buried his head in his hands. For an instant, Toria thought he might break down.

But she knew from the slight lines on his face and the dark intrigue of his eyes that he had faced adversity in his life. Many times. So many that his strength was increased as he struck down each new obstacle. A small-town English professor on the younger side of thirty didn't pose any threat, Toria thought ruefully.

"The Byleukrainian government wants me back. And the United States is happy to give me back if it will help their diplomatic relationship."

"When are you supposed to go?"

"Anya and I are to be deported next week. Without that green card, I have no options."

"So you're going to Byleukrainia?"

"No. I will lay down my life to make sure that never happens," he said in a choked voice.

"So where will you go?"

"We will have to...disappear," he answered cautiously. "America is a big country. Many people do that. All the time."

"What do you mean—disappear?"

"We will just..." He paused and snapped his fingers. "Disappear. To Chicago, which is nearby. Or maybe New York. Los Angeles. I've always wanted to live in a warm climate," he added with an insouciant shrug that was made poignant by the tragic circumstances he faced.

"What will you do?"

That shrug again. It didn't mean he didn't know. It meant he was being patient with her, warily telling her a few things because he thought she might be trustworthy. But not wanting to say too much, too much that could hurt him and his little girl.

NICK WAS an intensely private man, not used to sharing troubles. Especially not with doe-eyed beauties whom he worshipped from afar and wanted to kiss right up close.

He jerked his thoughts back to Anya.

Anya, the force that drove him to find a better life. The product of a brief romance, now the purpose of his life. He was a father first, a man second. Not a very good father, he was the first to admit.

By the time he got the hang of diapers, she was potty-trained. By the time he knew enough to buy her fancy dresses, she was wearing overalls. And now that he was just starting to get the hang of braiding her hair in less than twenty minutes without cursing—in Byleukrainian she mercifully couldn't understand—Anya was probably going to move on to some new challenge.

She had said something about all the other girls in her class getting an allowance....

Yes, he had to admit he wasn't the greatest dad. But he had gotten his daughter out of their troubled country. That was quite a feat. Now he'd do something even harder. He'd keep her out of that country.

"I'll get a job," he said, his accent barely there. "Maybe a cabbie. Busboy. Something that won't draw attention to myself."

"But not one as an environmental scientist with a multimillion-dollar research grant."

"Exactly. And I won't be a movie star."

"But it's a life on the run. Never secure. Never safe."

"It's better than the alternative."

"Why don't you appeal to the government?"

"You don't know much about this sort of thing," he said, not being unfriendly but merely pointing out her innocence. "I have exhausted every appeal available."

"And it's really so bad going back to...your country?"

"It's not my country anymore. America is my country. I want it for myself and for my daughter. But Byleukrainia wants me back. Badly. I am a scientist. They want to put me to work on arms research. I'd be very valuable to them in the laboratory and the political arena."

Toria gasped.

"I would refuse, of course," Nick continued. "They might...do things. But I would still refuse."

He saw shock register in her sherry-colored eyes. Americans so seldom understood the harsh realities of the world.

"What about Anya?"

"Ah, my little one. That's the reason I will never go back. I want to give her a good life. Byleukrainia is very backward—and like a firecracker about to explode. You read the newspapers, no?"

"Well, I haven't kept up with news from your country. It seems so confusing. So many groups fighting."

"Exactly. There is a constant battle for power and land. A government topples and a new one is formed. There is no stability. Would you want her to be sent back?"

Toria looked directly at him, and her even stare forced him to reconsider, however slightly, her delicacy. Perhaps within her there was a core of strength.

"No," she admitted. "I wouldn't want her sent back. She's so happy here. She's adjusted very well. No one would even know that she only came to America last spring."

"Exactly," Nick said, and for the first time his smile wasn't forced. "Children adjust very well to a good life."

He was heroic, even, in a quiet, thoughtful way that didn't involve guns and machismo.

What had Missy called him? A hunk? Not nearly as important a description as Dad. Although hunk would do nicely, as well.

What am I thinking of? She suddenly wondered, berating herself for being sidetracked. She was as bad as those overawed students who seemed to trail after him like disciples.

"So there's no alternative?" she pleaded.

He shook his head.

"But please always remember what a wonderful country you live in," he said wistfully. "You yourself have everything that I want to give my own daughter. An education. A home. Perhaps there are children you have?"

"No," Toria replied. "No children for me. Not yet. And not a husband. Yet."

"Oh," Nick said. "Well, I only hope that one day Anya will have what you have. America is truly a land of opportunity. It is possible."

They heard footsteps and Anya appeared at the door. Toria stood up and awkwardly gave Anya a hug. "Goodbye, my friend," she said. "Good luck."

Anya struggled to hold back her tears. "Goodbye, 'Fessor Toria."

Toria looked over at Nick from her embrace of his daughter. He studied them carefully, his eyes glittering like twin jewels. Then his lips tightened.

"Goodbye," he said gruffly. "I am sorry we troubled you with our problems. Just remember that you have a very nice life here in America. No matter what the problems are, they are very minor compared..."

He shrugged off the end of his sharp sentence. Toria felt reproached.

"Good luck," she said. "I hope..."

But she didn't know what she could hope for, what the Sankovitches could hope for, in a situation like this.

So she merely hugged Anya again, trying to squeeze into the girl all the love she felt—and then she quickly walked away.

Chapter Three

The quad was a half-acre cobblestone square bordered by ancient trees and the four academic buildings of North Central College. Toria waded through the brilliant carpet of leaves to a graying teak bench facing the library. The walk from the science building wasn't taxing, and yet she felt breathless.

As Toria explored her feelings, she realized that the little girl had become important—very important—to her in the past few months. So unsettling was the picture Nick painted of the two alternatives left to him and his daughter.

Life in Byleukrainia sounded even worse than life on the run in America. Anya and her father didn't deserve either.

Toria was lucky to live in circumstances that would never force her to make that kind of choice.

Still, she had felt patronized and somewhat off balance by Nick's lecture on how much she had.

Of course, he was right. That's part of what made his lecture so disturbing. She had her own home, the Victorian farmhouse just off campus, the very one she had grown up in. She had a wonderful teaching job where she really made a difference for her students. She had a circle of friends who were loyal and funny and empathetic. She certainly wasn't rich, but she had all the material comforts one could want.

Hers hadn't been a hard life—sure, there had been some difficult times, particularly when her parents had died within weeks of each other just as she was finishing her master's degree.

And then there was the persistent ache she often felt as she realized that because she was on the brink of thirty, her chances of being happily married and having children were fading. Not by much, she hastened to remind herself, but still . . .

Of course, there were plenty of women who found love, married and had families when they were in their thirties, even forties. Toria had just begun to hear the whisper of a possibility that such might not be her future. Her friends told her she was silly to wait for the perfect man. And she had always responded "Why shouldn't I?"

But as Toria became first bridesmaid to many and then godmother to more babies, she wondered if she was making a mistake waiting for a man who would make her heart leap into her throat, who was honorable and brave, who was romantic and sensitive.

A man as perfect as the cavalry officer who danced on top of the music box in her office.

Missing out on love and romance was her only real hardship—and yet she had bristled at Nick's lecture about the ease of American life.

Why? Not because she could disagree.

Maybe because he implied that she wasn't what he seemed to be: brave, hardy, careworn.

Maybe he disturbed her because she found him attractive—although she certainly didn't respond in that breathless, overtly sexual way Missy did.

What made him attractive? Not the casualness of his clothes and demeanor, the way his jeans hugged his hips and the damp, nearly sexual impression of sweat at the back of his shirt.

And most definitely not the tightness of his muscles and the predatory half-lidded way he appraised her.

Couldn't be. She had always been more attracted to men in tweed. Academicians. The wire-rimmed-glasses sort. Although, Toria admitted to herself, lately the scholarly look had started to...well, bore her.

Still, Nick wasn't her type. Wasn't her style.

Didn't matter, anyway.

Not in the least.

He was leaving.

That very night.

Toria picked up her briefcase, stood up and smoothed the nearly invisible wrinkles on her navy skirt.

Then she remembered she had left her exam key in her office. The exam key listed the twenty-odd concepts she wanted her students to explore—or at least mention—in their exams. If she was going to make any progress on grading those midterms this evening, she'd need that key.

She ran up the stairs and unlocked her office door, just as a gust of autumn wind lifted the lace curtains up to the ceiling. The familiar music of "The Black Forest Waltz" started to play.

She switched on the light and stared at the music box.

The few times the music box had begun playing on its own, Toria had chalked up to the fact that it was more than a hundred years old and its mechanisms were a little eccentric. But as she stood by the doorway, watching the dancers with the eerie backdrop of a late-September twilight, she was transfixed by the couple. Her briefcase slipped from her fingers and landed with a loud thud on the floor.

Could it be that she had never noticed a certain roguishness in the cavalry officer's face? A certain intensely masculine recklessness that couldn't possibly exist in an innocent porcelain lover? He was still an officer, but maybe not quite so much of a gentleman at this moment.

Then the tinkling music faltered and died. Toria decided she was just overwrought about the news of Nick and Anya's departure.

She quickly pulled down the window sash, straightened the curtains and picked up the exam key from her desk. Shoving it into her briefcase, she switched off the light and turned only once to look again at the music box on the window table.

The cavalry officer's eyes seemed to twinkle mockingly in the reflected light of the quad. She stepped closer to investigate.

Then it came to her: an idea so simple and so brilliant that she was surprised it hadn't occurred to her when she was sitting in Nick's office.

A warning voice in her head rapidly started listing dangers, but Toria shushed the doubts and rationales.

She had the perfect plan.

Now all she had to do was catch up to Nick and Anya before they disappeared into the night.

"NICK! ANYA! WAIT!"

Nick was loading boxes into the black pickup truck's bed. Anya sat in the front passenger seat, and she waved excitedly when she saw Toria.

Toria returned her little friend's greeting with enthusiasm but continued walking to the back of the truck. Nick stood, arms folded across his chest, his heavy eyelids making his expression completely unreadable under the streetlights.

"Nick, I just came up with an idea to keep you in the country legally," she said brightly.

He merely shook his head and reached down for another box. His flannel shirt pulled at his shoulders. As he stood up and shoved the box into the back of the pickup, he chuckled.

"Professor Tryon," he said. "You are so charming when you have ideas."

"Toria," she corrected him, ignoring his patronizing compliment.

"Toria," he said, lingering at the last syllable as if her name were a fine wine. "My attorney and I have come up with every conceivable angle known to immigration law. I find it hard to believe you would come up with something new."

"Well, you haven't thought of this one."

He looked at her from beneath his heavy eyebrows. Toria, even in her ever-so-sensible pumps, was still a good six inches shorter than he. Maybe that was what made him look so sure of himself, and so maddening.

"Haven't thought of this one? Really? I haven't? Not even my attorney?"

His derision might have made her back off, partly because he made her feel so young, so naive, so childish, and partly because he simply made her so darned angry, as if he had all the answers.

Anya had come out of the passenger side of the truck to put her arms around Toria. The hug reminded Toria how important it was that Nick and Anya stay in the country—legally. But getting Anya's hopes up with a plan that might, just might, not work would be cruel. Toria hesitated and then knew what to do.

"How about I buy you guys a cup of coffee at the student union?" she asked, gesturing at the red-brick building over Nick's shoulder.

"I don't like coffee," Anya said.

"All right. A soda," Toria suggested.

"Could I also have quarters for the video game?" Anya countered.

"Okay, okay, but only if it's all right with your dad."

Anya jumped up and down, tugging on Toria with supergirl strength.

Nick put his hands on his hips. "This is a really good idea?"

"Yes," Toria said defensively.

"Please! Please! Please!" Anya shrieked. "I haven't played Alien Forcefield in three days."

Nick grunted, hoisted three more boxes into the truck's bed, slammed the bed door and shrugged in the direction of the union.

Apparently, that shrug meant yes.

"Yippppeeee!" Anya cried out.

Nick fished in his jeans' pocket and pulled out a handful of change, which Anya swiped with practiced speed. As the adults silently walked from the parking lot, Anya raced ahead and dashed through the revolving doors.

Though Nick gave her no encouragement, Toria could barely contain her excitement at her idea as she followed him into the student union.

The warning voice that said this was trouble squawked and protested but was finally muffled by Toria's enthusiasm. *This is going to work, this is going to work!*

Nick sat at a booth near the video games but shielded from the main eating area by a set of booths. He acknowledged three students who called out his name, but he made clear with only the barest of nods that further conversation wasn't invited.

Toria brought them both foam cups of steaming black coffee from the help-yourself counter.

They smiled uncertainly at each other. "I didn't know what you take," she said.

"Doesn't matter."

Well, if my plan works out, it will matter, she thought to herself.

"So what's this great idea of yours?" Nick asked wearily. "You are a very charming and beautiful woman, and I am sorry that I have never had the opportunity to get to know you. Now, I have so much to do this evening if I am to get on my way. What is your...plan?"

"It's a proposal, really."

She hoped her use of the word "proposal" would prompt his thinking.

"And what is this proposal?" he asked.

"Well, that's what I'm doing now. Proposing."

His eyebrows came together. "You'll forgive me if my English isn't good enough for me to catch on immediately. A proposal is a plan or a proposition—" He stopped himself and looked her up and down.

That look again.

Toria felt a blush creeping across her face. His eyes widened and Toria noticed their color changed from blue to green. The green of spruce and pine, of forest and soft velvet. And a lazy, satisfied smile spread across his face, the bronzed skin on his flat, high cheekbones crinkling with mirth.

"Just what kind of proposition are you making me?"

Oh, no, Toria thought. *He thinks I'm seducing him.*

"It's entirely honorable," she said hastily. "I'm proposing...you know—marriage."

After she managed to get the M word out of her mouth, Toria realized what an effort this had been.

She felt her leg muscles relax, her shoulders drop a good six inches and her jaw untense enough for her to notice that it had been tense in the first place.

All this for Anya, she reminded herself.

And, for a moment, it looked as if he were the kindest, handsomest, most wonderful man on earth. Toria even thought she might like him. He was nice, almost lovable. She wanted to hug him.

Her plan was beginning to look better and better. It would work. Anya would stay in America. There would be so many more afternoons spent in her office. The days melted in her imagination into a puddle of homework sessions, snacks at the student union, quiet evenings at home playing checkers with the little girl....

But then he started to laugh. Heartily. Loudly. In that deeply Slavic way. In the way of a man who has found very little in the hardships of his life to celebrate, in the way of a man who grabs each instance of pleasure, however small and delicate.

"Marry?" he repeated, as tears of laughter filled his eyes.

Anya even stopped playing the Alien Forcefield game for an instant, a bare instant, to stare.

Toria thought she might like to seep into the brown acrylic carpet and disappear into its intricate pattern like a coffee stain.

Chapter Four

"I saw the movie *Green Card*," Toria said indignantly.

Nick stopped laughing.

"*Green Card*?"

"Gérard Dépardieu wants to stay in America and so he marries Andie MacDowell."

"And how does it end?"

Toria started to say and then stopped herself.

The movie hadn't ended well, if your measure of success was whether Dépardieu stayed in the country.

"I'm not going to spoil the ending for you," she said finally.

"If I'm lucky enough to stay in the United States, I promise I won't blame you if I ever see the movie," Nick said, and then he smiled wickedly. "And if I'm unlucky and end up in Byleukrainia, I can assure you they don't have any Blockbuster Video stores where I'm going."

"I still would feel funny," Toria said, and she played with the plastic spoon that had come with the coffee and then stopped because he was staring at her so intently. "Oh, all right, he screws up the interview with the Immigration and Naturalization Service and ends up being sent back to France."

"Ha! I rest my case," Nick said, slapping the tabletop. "Arranged marriages to fool the INS are very hard to pull off. My attorney had a woman... a professional, really, who was willing to try. For a price, she would be my bride for a year. But I thought I would win my case on the basis of the need for me to complete my environmental research. Now it's too late to build a convincing case of a marriage for love unless..." He paused, looked at her and then determinedly stared out the window.

"Unless what?" Toria asked.

He shook his head, refusing to answer or even to meet her gaze. Silence. Toria knew most people couldn't stand silence in conversation, but if she just waited quietly for a few seconds he would finish the sentence. He'd tell her.

What did he mean? That *unless* sounded like a possibility.

She counted the seconds in her head.

One, two, three...

She'd wait him out.

Ten, eleven, twelve...

What an infuriating man!

Nineteen, twenty, twenty-one...

"I've got it!" Toria exclaimed. "I know what you're thinking! A colleague! You can't backdate a courtship with anybody but a colleague, someone you've been seeing here at North Central. Nick, we're naturals. Two academics. We work at the same school. And though it's not really true, we could have bumped into each other every day at the library. Or at the faculty mailboxes. Or even at faculty meetings, even though I've only seen you at one."

Ignoring the chiding for failure to attend, Nick nodded only slightly. "I suppose what you say is true."

"We could have worked late together!" Toria added. "We could have seen each other in downtown Naperville. We could have... could have had coffee together every night at your office. Or mine, for that matter. And everyone, at least everyone in my department, knows Anya spends every afternoon with me. Nick, we really could have been ... you know, in love."

He shook his head at her triumphant finale. He had known she couldn't possibly have any new ideas, any real possibilities. He had agreed to sit down because he wanted just this—the chance to shore up his memories of a beautiful woman. His princess in the tower.

"You are so kind," he said, with a bittersweet mixture of sadness and admiration. "I nearly started to believe the same thing myself. But Toria, it wouldn't work. No one, least of all the INS, would ever believe we'd fall in love. We are too different. Even you can see we're not a match."

"And why not?"

He held up his hands—surely the answer was obvious.

"I've lived a life on the run, first from the Communists of my country and then from the dictators who have swept into power afterward. I'm a coarse man, nothing more than a peasant with a degree, and I don't have any patience with the finer things of life. And I don't want those finer things, anyway. You, on the other hand, *are* the finer things in life."

"What kind of finer things?"

He waved his hand in the air as he rattled off the things that no doubt made Toria's life worth living.

"Dainty lunches, plays with no plots, books to be put on coffee tables, eating off a plate that has a gold rim on it, and—" Nick paused as he searched for the most stunning indictment "—opera!" he finished. "I don't like opera. And I bet you love it."

"I don't go to the opera," she said. She pulled her shoulders inward at his scrutiny. "All right," she admitted. "My parents amassed a very large collection of opera recordings. I still listen to them sometimes."

He shrugged. "I told you so."

"But I don't understand any of the words," Toria added. "And I don't like the German ones with all that bellowing."

"Still, you are—what?—the daughter of two North Central professionals, the head librarian and the chairman of the linguistics department, and you live a life of culture and refinement. Too civilized, too fragile, too delicate for me."

"How do you know all that?"

"Anya has told me much about you."

"She has? Like what?"

"That you really do drink your tea from a cup and saucer. And use a silver spoon and an embroidered linen napkin. You keep all of this at your office so that you never have to use these kind of cups.''

She looked at the foam cups in front of them.

''So? Maybe I do it because, like you, I have a commitment to the environment. Foam takes up space in landfills.''

''You do it because you're trying your best to live your life in a beautiful and gracious manner.''

''So?''

''Anya also says you don't own a television set. I happen to think that *The Partridge Family* and *Gilligan's Island* represent two of the greatest examples of Western theater. You like—how do I say this?—'relationship' movies and I like Schwarzenegger. You haven't been to a McDonald's or a Burger King in years, and Anya and I would starve if it weren't for those two places. I love the twentieth century, and you wear tea-rose perfume as if you were a nineteenth-century heroine.''

''She never told you that last part.''

His face flushed and he looked out the window to the quiet suburban streets.

''She didn't have to.''

Toria swallowed as she understood the implications. He had noticed her. A tiny part of her was pleased. She worked to suppress that frisson of pleasure.

''So what's so bad about all that?'' she demanded, taking the offensive. ''What's so bad about being different from each other? After all, opposites attract.''

"Maybe they do, but then they crash—like magnets. No one, for an instant, would believe that you would fall in love with me. Or vice versa."

He punctuated his last words with a bang on the table that startled Toria.

"Vice versa?"

He shrugged. "I could love you from afar, but if I'm not courtly enough to get a first date with you, we could hardly fall in love."

"You've never asked," Toria pointed out.

"I'm talking theoretically."

"Theoretically, you could have."

He opened his mouth to say something, and then smiled, a sly courtly smile.

"I wish I would have known that months ago," he said. "I might have tried."

Suddenly, Toria realized they weren't talking theoretically anymore. This man was flirting with her! That hadn't happened in the longest time.

Get back to business, an inner voice ordered.

"So you think we can't get married?" she asked quietly.

"That's right."

"It can't be that difficult."

"Oh, it would be. Even if we come up with a convincing story for why we married, we'd still have to produce evidence of how our marriage thrives. We'd have to live together, learn about each other, know each other's quirks."

"It would be simple. I've had houseguests. I had roommates in college."

"Did you know what part of your roommate's body quivered at the slightest caress?"

"Certainly not!"

"Then you can see that this would not work. Being married is different, so different from any friendship or business relationship."

"Have you ever been married?"

"No," he said flatly.

"How did Anya ... ?"

"Long story. If we ever did get married, I'd tell you."

"Well, then I guess I won't ever hear it," Toria said. "Nick, I'm sorry that you have to go on the run. I want you to know that if I were making the rules, you'd have a permanent spot in this country. I'm sorry if I wasted your time with my silly idea."

She noticed he wasn't looking at her anymore. She followed his intent gaze to the little girl at the video game. Anya was lost in a world where she was the pilot of a spaceship evading a battalion of rockets. Anya was good, but the game was better—when she lost, though, she had a second chance. Many second chances, if the row of quarters she had neatly stacked in front of her were any indication.

Toria looked at her coffee. It was too painful to look at her little friend, knowing that she was so soon to be snatched from her. She would miss Anya, and Toria again wondered what kind of life it would be for them on the run.

Nick would never be able to offer Anya the advantages she had being the daughter of a professor. The steady income, the security of living in one place, the college town's emphasis on learning and education and the sureness of her safety.

The occasional high-tech explosion from the game and Anya's delighted shrieks punctuated the relative quiet of the room.

Nick said something just as Anya screamed in victory.

"What?" Toria asked, barely concealing her grief.

"I said I would be very honored to accept your offer of marriage," he said quietly.

His eyes welled with tears, but he quickly and brutally brushed them away just as Toria was about to reach out to him. She put her hand back on her lap as if she had been about to be burned.

"You have offered me a way to give my child a better life," he added soberly. "I cannot refuse. I can't decline to take a chance that might make a difference. I must do everything—however outrageous, however unlikely to succeed, however plain crazy. I must try everything."

"Including marrying me?"

He smiled, appreciating her attempt to lighten up the reality of their venture.

"Yes, even marrying you," he said, sighing dramatically. "But please do not make me eat this bran stuff Anya says you have every morning for breakfast. I bought a box to satisfy her curiosity and it tastes like cardboard. I prefer to pick up an Egg McMuffin on the way into the office."

As Nick watched her smile, more from relief than from his humor, he wondered what it would be like to reach across the Formica table and yank the ribbon from her blouse's high, stiff collar. His hands ached to touch her, to rub against the softness of her skin: her cheeks, her neck, down to her breasts—damnably armored not just by a blouse but by a suit jacket styled so much like a man's.

"Would we...sleep together?" he asked, his voice husky. He coughed to clear his throat and took a sip of the bracing coffee.

He smiled tenderly at the naive shock that registered on her face, though he knew it might be dangerous to push this woman who might save his daughter's future. He had to know, though. How far she was willing to go.

"Of course not," Toria said. "I have two guest rooms. Besides, wouldn't it be wrong with Anya...?"

He thought carefully.

"If we went forward with your proposal, I would tell Anya we are marrying because we love each other. It would be safer than involving her in a lie. Because, after all, what we would be doing is a nothing less than the biggest lie either of us have ever told."

"I'm not very good at lying."

"I'm not, either. But when my daughter's safety is at stake, I can get good at it. I just don't think she needs to learn."

"Well, then you had better tell her that we are a couple who believes in separate bedrooms," Toria said crisply.

"I think sleeping together would be better, but I'm willing to try it this way. If those are your rules."

"They are. I'm not the kind of woman..." She struggled to find the words.

Nick shook his head. "You don't have to say."

"And let's agree right now that we'll be . . . friends and nothing more," Toria added. "Don't try anything. If you're doing this for Anya, you'll respect my rules."

"I will. Besides, if you want me, I won't need to do anything. You'll just tell me you want me."

"What?" Toria asked, recoiling.

"I'm just saying if you want me you'll tell me. American women are very . . ."

"Very what?" Toria demanded.

He held out his hands as if he were searching for the right English word. But he knew exactly what he was thinking of.

Okay, so maybe Toria wasn't like that.

She stared at him.

He looked away uncomfortably.

"Byleukrainian women are more . . . restrained," he said finally, not satisfied with the word he used and was instantly aware he had chosen the wrong one.

He felt terrible. The woman he considered most out of reach sat before him and he couldn't find the words to tell her that he wouldn't overstep any boundaries she might set up. But that if only she were to say the word . . .

"American women, when they want a man, they just tell him," he said, snapping his fingers. "And that is that. If you want me, you will do the same."

From the horrified look on her face, he knew he was digging himself in deeper and that he should shut up while he hadn't yet been slapped.

It wasn't quite true that American women always told a man when they wanted him. No, some women had said it to him with their eyes, their whisper, their look.

"You're very sexist," she accused tartly.

"Not sexist, just realistic."

Tightening her lips with disapproval, she started in the direction of Anya when Nick's arm shot out and grabbed hers.

"Please remember," he said gruffly, and then quickly softened his tone as he realized that if he frightened or upset her too much, she might back out of helping him, helping Anya. "Please remember, we're supposed to be in love."

She looked down at where he gripped her arm. He let go. The wrinkled fabric of the sleeve of her navy jacket reminded them both of his intensity.

"Sorry," he said. "My beloved."

She blanched at his words of endearment and looked like a small, tender animal trapped in the sights of a hunter's gun.

"It's all right, Nick," she said, recovering, feeling his name so strange upon her tongue. "Beloved."

Chapter Five

"You may kiss the bride."

Toria snapped to attention, her heart stuck in her throat, her ears ringing, her fingers trembling.

She looked at the judge, who stared implacably at the clock hanging on the wall over the door. She looked at Anya, solemnly holding aloft a bouquet of seasonal wildflowers. She looked down at her own left hand, now adorned with an intricately patterned band of gold that had once belonged to Nick's grandmother.

She forced herself to look at Nick.

As her eyes met his, she suddenly wanted to run, to scream, to hide.

What was she doing? she thought wildly. What had ever possessed her to so impulsively marry a man she didn't know? She wasn't even the kind of person who bought the items near the register at the grocery store.

It wasn't that she hadn't thought about Nick and Anya after the trio had said their goodbyes the previous evening.

She had thought of nothing else.

But in the safety of her home, surrounded by familiar things, she had focused only on practical matters. Like whether there were enough guest towels. Like finding the extra set of sheets for the twin bed Anya would use. Like vacuuming with a zeal she never knew she possessed—catching even the errant dust balls under the heavy armoires in the bedrooms. She had even gone to CeeBee Groceries at 2:00 a.m., stocking up on kids' cereals for Anya and sodas for Nick.

Staring at the beer display, thinking that she hadn't had a man in her house for more than a year. And that man had been the UPS deliveryman toting packages.

She had decided she could ask Nick if he wanted beer and come back later if he did.

But these eminently practical matters—even scrubbing the bathroom and taking down the panty hose drying on the towel rack—had been a distraction.

And when she had thought about this wedding at all, it had only been with barely suppressed joy about how wonderful it was to ensure Anya's safety and how great it would be to spend more time with her.

Little did she know that from the very first words of the ceremony, the solemnity of the occasion would effect its own changes in her.

That the sacred promises would ring true.

Had she just now promised to love, honor and cherish this man for richer, for poorer?

"I do," she had said.

"In sickness and in health?" the judge had asked.

"I do."

"Till Death do you part?"

"I do," she had said.

And, being the woman she was, she couldn't say those words without meaning them.

The judge cleared his throat. Nick stared questioningly at her from beneath heavy, shadowy lids. Anya hopped on one foot and then another.

Toria opened her mouth as if to say something. As if to explain. As if she could.

She was getting married.

A big deal.

It was a big sacred deal, as a matter of fact.

And she was quite surprised.

The night before, she hadn't even known the words of the ceremony. But whether said by a holy man in an ancient cathedral, a justice of the peace in a roadside chapel, or here in the county courthouse with a ceremony performed by an indifferent judge, wedding vows changed a woman.

Wedding vows made a woman a part of a couple.

She was Nick's wife.

Regardless of what happened with the INS, regardless of where their lives took them, she would always be his wife. His woman. His. And somehow she had ended up with him. He was her husband. Her man. Hers.

She hoped this feeling would pass, like some fleeting case of indigestion. Quickly. Because if it didn't she would be in a lot of trouble.

She was certain Nick felt none of this.

His concern was merely with eluding deportation. But now, as he stared at her, his eyes widened slightly and the muscles of his strong jaw clenched—he looked worried. Her hesitation must have made him think she was going to back out on him.

She jutted out her chin, swallowed hard and licked her lips to stop their trembling. She glanced at Anya, reminding herself of the true purpose of this wedding.

Nick reached out to her shoulder, touching her first with delicacy and then with growing possessiveness. Drawing her to him with growing confidence.

She looked into his eyes. He had to know that she felt she was his, all his. Bound to him by an agreement she had made without comprehension. Could he have been so consumed with worries about deportation that he hadn't noticed?

She closed her eyes as he brought his mouth to hers.

She knew she was making a big mistake—no use wishing it weren't so.

It was a mistake to say "I do" unless you meant it.

She was like a china doll, so delicate that he feared she might break in his callused hands. All the scrubbing he had done after the morning's fieldwork in preparation for his wedding couldn't wash away the sensation that he was too coarse for her.

He touched her shoulder, rousing her from her worry, her concern. No doubt she was thinking of the English department's faculty meeting she had said was scheduled for just fifteen minutes from now.

If they hurried, they could get back to campus...

Hurried? Nick groaned.

He had never thought his wedding day would be like this.

As a man, he hadn't thought about it too much. Not like girls with their fantasies of gowns and flowers and bridesmaids and parties. But he had always assumed, watching the men of his village, that he would marry in the traditional way. He closed his eyes.

The smell of the incense the priest shook over the couple. The solemnity of the ancient vows. And then, the crackle and hiss of the logs on the wedding bonfire that would burn for days. The women's brightly patterned skirts twirling and whirling as they danced. The taste of hearty wine and spicy food. The shouts of the men as they hoisted bride and groom on their shoulders for a triumphant march through the streets.

Ah, Americans are so practical, Nick thought as he looked at his new bride.

A courthouse.

A judge.

A license.

A twenty-five-dollar check, made payable to the Office of the Clerk of the DuPage County.

In ten minutes, it was over.

He brought her to him, torn between gratitude that she would help him, coupled with an oddly primitive swelling of masculine pride and possessiveness. He would have to remind himself she was not truly his bride.

And yet, the judge had just told him to kiss her.

A kiss to seal their bargain and their fates, as the handshake of the previous night could not do.

He leaned over, willing her rosebud lips to open to him.

Their mouths touched with the finest brush of skin against skin. As delicate as the wings of a butterfly or the feathers of a newly hatched bird.

He opened his eyes and looked into her startled golden gaze. He should stop. They had satisfied the requirements of an American wedding ceremony. It was enough.

But by some force he could not name, his mouth pressed again upon hers. His arms caught her up, startling them both with his vigor. He took her mouth, possessing it as surely as if she were really, truly his. A touch of her prim indignation—so piquant—quickly melted to surrender.

And he just as suddenly relinquished her, nearly shoving her away from him as if in distaste, but truly in fear of his own pleasure, his own quick-fire desire.

He couldn't hold her. He couldn't touch her. Couldn't take her into his arms merely for show. If he did, he wouldn't stop with just one kiss.

Every muscle tensed, he was as swollen and on edge as if he had spent a night of lovemaking without release. Instead, it had been just one kiss.

One kiss cut short by his own honor and self-discipline. And by the presence of his daughter and an impatient judge.

You are my woman. The haunting Byleukrainian wedding promises intruded into the modern courtroom. *You are my woman forever.* And with that thought, his eyes met hers.

He remembered every word of the vows, heard so many times at so many village weddings. And now, with an act of will, he had to shake them from his head.

She is not your wife! His inner voice roared.

And yet, she stood before him—to all appearances, no different from any other bride—nervous and flushed, as his wife.

"Congratulations," the judge said, grabbing Nick's hand heartily. He put his other hand on Toria's shoulder and guided the couple toward the courtroom door. "On behalf of the people of DuPage County, I want to wish you a long and happy marriage. Next, please."

"I CAN'T BELIEVE you two are married," Anya giggled excitedly as they walked out into the crowded hall. "I can't believe I never figured it out. It's just like a fairy tale. It's so romantic. I brought you together, sort of, didn't I?"

"You sure did," Toria said. *More than you could ever know,* she thought guiltily. It was a bad thing to lie. Especially to a child.

With a heavy heart, she thought of the deception she was embarking upon. She would be lying to everyone. Her colleagues. Her students. The government. The only thing stopping her from lying to her parents was that they were already gone.

Her eyes met Nick's. His gaze was possessive, in an open way that no man had ever dared look at her. Or maybe she just imagined what he was thinking. Maybe he was only as nervous as she.

No, no, that glint of masculine appraisal was unmistakable, as mixed as it was with gratitude for the help that she was giving and would give him.

She felt unsteady, and could not muster the indignation that would put any civilized man in his place. And though she steadily held his gaze, her heart fluttered like a moth captured in closed hands.

"I'm sorry," he said abruptly, softly so that Anya would not hear. "Not about marrying you, but I shouldn't have kissed you like that. Are you furious with me?"

She shook her head, thinking again that they had embarked on a journey, a mysterious journey others had taken before them. They hadn't anticipated the subtle shifts of emotion and the power of age-old rituals, hadn't thought through the deceptions to come.

"It's my fault," she said, in a barely there whisper. "I'm the one who proposed."

"Regrets?" he whispered in her ear.

"None," she said firmly. "I am the one who got us into this."

She was the one who, in the safety of her Victorian farmhouse last night, had thought the marriage would have all the hallmarks of entertaining a few houseguests for the season. Suddenly the question of whether to put the linen hand towels in the guest bathroom didn't seem quite so important. She could have just kicked herself.

Nick picked up three extra copies of the marriage certificate from the county clerk. While waiting with Toria, Anya asked if she could keep the bouquet of Queen Anne's lace and late-blooming black-eyed Susans that Nick had picked that morning on the banks of the DuPage River. He had given them to Toria sheepishly when they had met at the quad, saying that he had spent the morning collecting water samples for his field study.

"Weddings are so romantic," Anya mused dreamily. "You two are just like the couple on the music box."

"The music box in my office?"

"Yeah. You're like the woman, all beautiful and delicate and Dad's just like the officer. Brave and heroic."

As Anya started humming, Toria looked down at her no-nonsense blazer and crisp white blouse. She ordinarily didn't dress up, preferring long, soft skirts and comfortable sweaters. But in honor of this ceremony, she had chosen the suit from her wardrobe, the navy suit she wore to the once-yearly meeting of the full faculty senate.

She certainly didn't look like the porcelain woman on her music box.

She glanced at Nick, whose back was turned as he leaned over the clerk's counter. His blue-black hair fell on his forehead—a good two weeks overdue for a haircut, Toria noted. He wore a white button-down shirt, in obvious deference to the occasion, and had even paired it with a blue silk tie.

But Nick was, as always, his own man, a man who valued his work and his comfort. His fingers were callused and his jeans clean but worn. The slightest traces of dirt remained on his work boots. Hardly cavalry-officer material.

But still, it was sweet for Anya to think of them as romantic.

"You're a very sweet girl," Toria observed, hugging her new daughter. "I hadn't noticed that your father and I are like that."

"Oh, but you are!"

"I'm glad you're a romantic, Anya."

"I'm not a real romantic," Anya protested, pulling a face. "You know I hate boys. But I like you guys being romantic. I'm so happy you're married."

"You really are?" Toria asked, suddenly realizing it would have been perfectly understandable if Anya's feelings for Toria had shifted dramatically as Toria changed from being a friend to being... a seeming rival for her father's affections. But Anya's enthusiasm quickly dispelled that worry.

"I'm superexcited!" Anya exclaimed. "You can't have a home without a mom, and I haven't had a home in a long, long time."

Toria closed her eyes, smelling Anya's scent of Ivory soap and jelly beans. She had to fight back tears—what a life this girl has lived so far, she thought, to find her stability in Toria.

And yet, I'm the one who needs a home. Only hours before, she had frantically, but happily, prepared her house for her guests—her new husband and daughter. Even vacuuming hadn't been the usual excruciating torture. Besides, you can't have a home without—

She looked up, starting at Nick's gentle touch at her shoulder. She got the impression that he had been observing the private moment between her and Anya.

"Ready to go?" he asked hoarsely.

Toria nodded, pulling away from Anya. But instead of relinquishing Toria, Anya clung tighter and drew her father into the embrace.

Embarrassed, Toria turned her head away from his. She found the intimacy, even a brief embrace, disconcerting.

Out of the corner of her eye she saw a flicker of movement. She looked across the bustling corridor, filled with nervous brides and grooms, wary litigants, lawyers, police and court officials. A bald man in a gray suit leaned against the wall, a cigarette hanging from his mouth in defiance of the No Smoking sign posted behind his head.

He stared at Toria, brazenly intruding on the privacy one can often find in the most crowded, public areas. His eyes narrowed with hostility.

Toria suddenly realized that everything she did from now on, everything that Nick did, might be observed.

By someone. Anyone.

And anyone could blow their cover.

This man, with his small black eyes, made her shiver with fear.

"Nick?" she asked in a choked voice.

"What?"

He had leaned down to accept his daughter's embrace. His hair had fallen across his face so she couldn't read his expression, but she wanted to communicate to him. Her fears. Her worries. Her dawning realization of the difficulty of their deception—difficulty that he must have long since realized.

No wonder he hadn't tried this before, even aside from his misgivings about deceit.

She put her hand on his shoulder, startling him with her touch.

"Nothing," she said.

He looked down at her and mouthed the words "Thank you."

She smiled tremulously, not trusting the moment.

Anya pulled away. Their reason for touching gone, Toria and Nick let go of each other.

"I'm hungry. When are we going to have lunch?" Anya asked.

"Toria has a faculty meeting she's late for," Nick said. "But if you want me to stop at the drive-through window at Lenny's..."

"Lenny's?" Toria cried. "You must be kidding."

"The hot-dog stand," Nick explained.

"I know what it is. It's just, so...greasy. Do you eat there often?"

"All the time," Anya said cheerfully.

Nick shrugged. "I'm not very good at cooking," he said apologetically.

"How will we celebrate the wedding?" Anya cried out, horrified.

"I've planned a nice quiet dinner," Toria said. "A quiche, some fruit salad, and..."

"Is there cake?" Anya demanded. "There can't be a wedding without cake."

"Of course there's cake," Toria said, making a note to stop at the bakery that afternoon.

"Let's go," Nick said. "We don't want you to be late for that meeting."

They headed down the corridor toward the exit to the parking lot. Nick slipped his hand underneath Toria's elbow. Away from the solemn courtroom, it seemed natural, even expected.

When she looked back at the spot where the unsettling observer had been, there was nothing but a stamped-out cigarette butt on the floor.

Chapter Six

"Doesn't it seem quiet to you?" Toria asked, as they parked Nick's pickup truck in the lot next to the quad.

"Yeah. Too quiet," Nick agreed.

"Where is everybody?" Toria wondered. She unbuckled her seat belt. "I've never seen the quad without any people in it."

Anya popped the last bite of her hot dog into her mouth, licked the ketchup from her fingers and followed Toria out the passenger door.

"Maybe everyone's at Toria's meeting," she said.

"Not likely," Toria said. "Sometimes I feel like I'm the only one who takes the English department's meetings seriously. At the last one, the chairman and I were the only people there. And he fell asleep after reading the minutes of the last one."

"I hate meetings," Nick said. He lifted the crate with his soil and water samples from the flatbed. "Why do you bother if no one else does?"

"I feel it's my duty," Toria said. Her words came out wrong, sounding more prim and pious than she meant. "I really believe in my work," she added.

"I'm the first taste of college these kids get, the first chance to get serious about their minds, the only opportunity some will get to catch up to their peers. And I feel very strongly that our English department is very good."

"And you want to meet with colleagues who get their thrills analyzing other people's footnotes and tearing apart novels they couldn't write?"

"I wouldn't put it quite so strongly."

He stopped, leaning his crate against the base of the statue of the college's former dean. Normally the statue would have been surrounded by students hanging out between classes.

"No, you wouldn't put anything that strongly, would you?"

"Is that a criticism?"

"Not at all," he said, his smile crinkling his eyes. "You are much nicer than that. And you are very dutiful to go to meetings."

"Don't you have the concept of 'duty' in Byleukrainia?"

"Of course. A man's duty is to his family and to his village. To care for the weakest and shield the young. Toria, I happen to think that honor is only for those who survive."

"That sounds like the beginning of some medieval knight's tale."

"No, I just mean meetings don't count for much with me," he said, eyes twinkling like jewels. "On the other hand, do you think the Knights of King Arthur's court would have lasted very long if they spent most of their days conferring?"

"With portable phones and electronic day-planners?" Toria teased, completing the vision. "I guess you're right. But you're not a knight. You're a respected scientist. What you should do for the sake of duty is different."

"Maybe so. But if you think about it, what I do now is not much different from what I would do if I were back in Byleukrainia. I'm protecting the land with research and technology instead of weapons."

"You feel very strongly about your work," Toria pointed out.

"Just as strongly as you do."

"Dad!" Anya shrieked. "Toria! Look! Balloons!"

They looked beyond Anya to the windows of the science building. Hundreds of white and pink balloons clung to the ceiling of the lecture hall. From the sidewalk, Toria couldn't see whether the hall was full, but she had a feeling that she knew where the crowd that hung out at the quad was.

"If they're having a party, can I go?" Anya asked, coming over and shyly slipping her hand in Toria's. Toria heard the longing in her voice.

"Sure, sweetheart, but I don't know that we've been invited. It probably has nothing to do with us. The college throws a big party every year to commemorate Dean Richard Eastman's birthday, but—come to think of it—that's not till next month. Maybe somebody's had a birthday or a shower or a..."

She looked over at Nick, mouth open in horror.

"You don't think somebody...?"

Nick hoisted the field-samples crate over his shoulder and led them toward the science building entrance.

"I did tell my secretary I was getting married this afternoon."

"You did?" Toria cried.

She took a deep breath and tried to think rationally. Of course, if somebody else in the English department had gotten married, she would be the one blowing up balloons for a college bash. When the chairman's wife had a baby, Toria had organized a shower. And for departmental birthdays, everyone could count on Toria to schedule lunch.

So why should it be any different when she got married?

Yet the prospect of walking into a room with the people she had worked with, studied with and taught with for nearly all her life was suddenly very scary.

"I told her I was doing a field study of the DuPage River until eleven," Nick explained, seemingly oblivious to her terror. "I said I would stop at the animal hospital to check on the orphaned raccoons I found last week. I'd get married around noon. And be back by one. I explained we loved each other but wanted to keep things low-key. And then I said I'd spend the rest of the afternoon in my office, and if students needed help on their research projects, they could schedule appointments for then."

Spoken like a true man, Toria thought wryly. True love slipped into the sentence between animal hospitals and office hours.

He turned and regarded Toria thoughtfully. "We had to tell people sooner or later."

"I know," Toria said. "But I thought we'd just send out announcements."

"Engraved ones, huh?" Nick teased. "My secretary organizes a party for every possible celebration in the environmental sciences department—baby showers, promotions, somebody publishing their first scholarly article. She must have thought this was the kind of thing that called for a party."

"It looks like a big one," Anya observed, hopping from foot to foot, clearly ready to bolt for the party at the slightest encouragement. "You should be happy. Everyone gets a party when they get married."

"They do," Nick agreed. "Now run on ahead. There's an old Byleukrainian custom that when the wedding couple comes to the wedding dinner a messenger must be sent ahead to tell the guests. So go warn the guests!"

Anya hesitated, but Toria smiled her encouragement and the girl shot off, taking the science-building steps two at a time.

"Now I know why the English department was having an 'emergency meeting,'" Toria said. "There wasn't any emergency. And no meeting, either. Your secretary must have called our department—"

"And they told you there was a meeting this afternoon because they know you, of all people, will show up for meetings," Nick said, completing her thoughts.

"They know me pretty well, don't they?"

"They do. What if they had said, 'We're having a party for you'?"

"I would have been too embarrassed."

"Why?"

"Because I'm lying. They think I'm married."

"You are."

"You know what I mean."

"I'm sorry."

"I never thought about how I'd have to face every one of my colleagues, every one of my students," Toria admitted.

"It will be tough," Nick conceded. "Always a deception. It will be a lonely one, too—we can't confide in our friends because any one of them might end up being questioned by the INS. You and I have to be the only ones who know."

Toria nodded dismally, staring at the party balloons rustling at the ceiling. "I hate lying," she said. "I don't feel very good about this."

"I know."

"I didn't think about all the little lies I'd have to tell every day. I didn't think about lying to my colleagues. Somehow I thought our marriage would be a private thing."

"If you want to back out, just say the word," Nick offered. "It's a little late, but we could pretend we're from Hollywood. Quickie divorce? Irreconcilable differences, friends forever, that kind of thing?"

"No," Toria said quickly, her dimpled chin trembling as she held it high. "I made you a promise. For Anya's sake."

"And I am grateful for that," Nick said softly. "Thank you forever."

They shared a smile, looking to the celebrants at the auditorium window like a couple in love. Toria noted a few people from her department, some students as well, crowding at the window to gawk.

"Kiss me," she said impulsively. She tilted her chin toward the window.

He knew—and didn't have to turn around to know that they were noticed.

He put down his crate and drew her into his embrace. "I'm going to have to make it look good," he warned.

"I know."

"Real good."

She closed her eyes.

"Try not to look as if you're terrified of me," Nick said.

She opened her eyes and smiled at his gentle rebuke.

He captured her then, a gentle hunter certain of himself and of the moment. His arms tugged her to him playfully and yet with masculine command. His mouth caught the honey-sweet essence of her smile. She startled, and yet, well aware of their audience, accepted his arms and followed his lead in presenting the drama of courtship and delight of new love.

Her heart beat against his chest, and he thought, for the briefest moment, that he was the happiest man on earth. He had his bride. The princess in the tower, the one he thought he'd never see again. Now his. His love for life. And yet, of course, she wasn't. Wasn't his bride, his princess, his love. But still, a man could dream.

Applause, whistles, and catcalls erupted from behind the auditorium window as they broke apart. Toria bit her lip, bringing a rich flush to her mouth. Nick groaned.

He touched her jaw with his roughened hand and brushed away his kiss with a gentle stroke of his thumb against her lips.

"Nick . . . ?" she whispered.

His thumb pressed firmly on her mouth.

"Shhh," he said softly. He took a deep breath and clenched his jaws tight, using every ounce of self-discipline he could muster to keep himself from crushing her tender lips with his, from picking her up and carrying her away much like a Byleukrainian warrior would take his bride.

"We should go in," Toria said.

"Yes, we should," he agreed hoarsely.

As he picked up his crate, Toria waved to the people standing at the window. She laughed brightly and Nick loved the sound, hoped he'd hear it a few more times as a memory of this happy moment. He guessed that her mirth hid a confused and tangled mix of emotions.

"After you, Mrs. Sankovitch," he said gently.

Her smile faltered for an instant at the sound of her married name, and Nick realized she'd need time before the name would feel natural. He only hoped they had enough time. It would take him a lifetime to get used to her not being Mrs. Sankovitch.

"HOW DID YOU EVER end up with him?" Missy Schroeder whispered after a shriek of congratulations and a bone-crushing hug. "You, of all women."

"What does that mean?" Toria asked, wondering frantically if Missy suspected the truth.

After all, Missy was the most notorious gossip on campus. If she discovered that the marriage was a sham, half of Naperville would be discussing the deception at their dinner tables that evening.

"Missy, we just tried to be discreet."

"I'm not talking about that—although I'm pretty furious at you for not telling me. No, I'm talking about why you ever fell in love. I mean, you two are so different I can't believe you ever got together," Missy said, flipping her wild, permed mass of red hair in a sexy gesture that promptly captured the attention of every male in the room. "You're so...proper."

While Missy congratulated herself on the perfect choice of words, Toria squirmed.

Proper?

That sounded so dismally boring. She wondered if others thought of her the same way.

"And Nick?" Toria queried. "Why can't you believe he'd fall in love with me?"

Missy closed her eyes and flicked her tongue over her brilliant ruby lips.

"He's so deliciously primitive."

"Primitive?"

"Primitive," Missy repeated languorously, as if the word itself was the naughtiest and sexiest way to describe a man. "That man must have a lot of...needs, if you get my drift. Toria, I never thought of you as

the type—but maybe I just don't know the real Toria
Tryon—I mean, Sankovitch. How'd you two get together? And how did you manage to keep it a secret
from me, your very best girlfriend?''

Toria shivered, though the room was hot and
packed with people. She looked about frantically for
Nick. If nosy people were going to start asking questions, they'd better get their stories straight.

"I'll agree with that assessment of our Byleukrainian colleague,'' Professor Ronald Dickson said.
Ronald did research on pre-Columbian literature that
nobody understood. He leaned over Missy's shoulder and grinned at Toria. "Primitive. Absolutely
primitive. A man with a lot of Old World machismo.
I can't imagine a more strikingly opposite couple. I
mean, I wouldn't think the Mayfair Hotel holds tea
parties on the swampy banks of the DuPage River. Or
that Nick here would be allowed in your house with
muddy hip boots.''

Missy giggled. "He's a hunk, I told you,'' she said,
shaking her finger at Toria. "Definite hunk material. You're not going to get any sleep between now
and the rest of your life. But you probably know that
already.''

Toria smiled shyly at her friend's teasing.

"So, go ahead and tell us,'' Missy urged Toria. "I
mean, every woman on campus would have been delighted to let Nick into her bedroom—hip boots or
not. When did you two first meet?''

Toria swallowed. She could hardly tell the truth—
last night.

"At the Dean's cocktail party in June," a hearty voice declared.

Toria turned around, relieved as Nick slipped his arm around her shoulder. She made quick introductions, ignoring Missy's frankly sexual appraisal of Nick.

"Dean Nash's cocktail party?" Ronald persisted. "You mean that ghastly 'do' where he gives that pep talk about how happy he is to be the head of such a wonderful college? And we all cringe because we just want to go home?"

"Speak for yourself," Toria said. "I always liked that party."

"And now I have a special reason for loving that party," Nick said, missing or purposely ignoring Ronald's derisive tone. "I was a little nervous about going, this year being my first as a faculty member. Remember? They held it in the courtyard because the rain had just stopped that afternoon. And I will remember forever walking down the brick path from the French doors and seeing Toria in that blue chiffon dress with the tiny white dots."

Missy's and Ronald's mouths hung open.

"Go on," Ronald encouraged.

"Toria had her hair pulled back with a blue headband and she wore tiny pearl earrings," Nick continued. He pulled Toria's hair back to show what he meant. "She's wearing them today. Don't they look beautiful on her delicate earlobes?"

Toria stared at Nick as her mind quickly reviewed the long-ago party.

How had he done it? How had he managed to remember this? And with such detail! And making her sound so...beautiful, when she would only have conceded she looked well-groomed.

Because, as she remembered the party, she knew he was absolutely right. She had worn her navy blue dress with the tiny dots. She had certainly worn her pearl earrings, a final gift from her mother, since she almost always did. And a headband? Toria couldn't remember for sure, but it sounded right.

"Tea rose," Nick said abruptly.

"Huh?" Ronald asked.

"Tea rose," Nick repeated. "That's what did it to me. She was wearing tea-rose perfume. I noticed it as I stood near her. And though I didn't have the courage to approach her then, I knew that I would make her my bride one day."

Missy sighed. "The whole story's so romantic. Makes me think next year I might enjoy the party. Maybe something like that will happen to me."

Ronald leaned closer to Toria. "Tea rose," he mused. "Yes, it's beautiful. Alluring, in a subtle, classy way. Yes, very alluring."

Nick touched Ronald's shoulder. "She's mine, Professor," he said, with just an undercurrent of quiet force.

Ronald looked down at the hand gripping his shoulder. Toria's face flushed. She looked away, glad to see that none of the other party-goers had noticed the challenge pass between the two men.

Ronald was the first to back off, shrugging out from under Nick's grip and smiling archly.

"A bit territorial, isn't he?" he quipped. "But cavemen always are." He held up his half-empty drink. "I think I'll retreat to the punch bowl," he said. "Come along, Missy. I was hoping we could talk about that research paper you circulated last week."

With a thumbs-up to Toria, Missy followed him, no doubt excited to find someone who would be interested in her analysis of the letters of Jane Austen.

"I think he meant 'territorial' as an insult," Nick said as they left. "As a modern American woman, you must feel the same way. Please understand that I am clumsy at your customs. Where I come from, a man does not want another man to have such intimacies with his wife."

"Even smelling her perfume?" Toria challenged.

"I embarrassed you, didn't I?" Nick asked with boyish earnestness.

"Yes, you did. Even if we were married for real," she whispered, "I wouldn't want you to say things like that. A wife is not property."

Nick felt a familiar conflict welling within him. The traditional ideas he grew up with—the ones that shaped him, molded him into manhood—versus the modern American openness and freedom.

If he wanted America's liberty for himself, he could hardly deny it to his bride. Yet he didn't like Ronald's making any suggestive comments about Toria. It was a challenge—a challenge from the tweedy type of academic that Toria was no doubt attracted to. The kind of academic who could have claimed her as his own if she hadn't taken it into her head to do Nick and Anya a favor.

Maybe it was jealousy that gnawed at him. Jealousy wasn't really part of any particular customs. That crossed all cultural barriers, he knew.

"I'm sorry," he said, though the words were hard to say, as all true apologies are. "I will try to remember that you are your own person."

"We'll work on it together," she said. "It'll take some time to get used to each other and accommodate each other."

She smiled, a delicate opening to her soul so precious that he had to remind himself that she wasn't truly his wife. Their partnership would only last as long as it took for the INS to grant him a new visa. Just long enough to ensure his daughter's safety.

"Come on, let's go find Anya," he said. "I haven't seen her since we got here."

He slipped his hand into hers, cautioning himself not to take too much pleasure from the way she leaned against him as he maneuvered through the crowd.

"By the way," she whispered, "how did you remember what I was wearing three months ago at an honestly boring and way too formal party?"

He felt the tiniest clutch in his chest, as if he had been found out. As if he had been caught at something his heart had tried to forget.

"I remember everything," he said cryptically. He was unwilling to commit himself to telling her that there was nothing else about that night that he could recall.

Chapter Seven

"Well, here it is," Toria said, unlocking the front door. "Welcome to your new home."

Nick's hand shot across the doorjamb, blocking her way.

Startled, Toria gasped.

"I should carry you across the threshold," he explained.

"Yeah!" Anya cried, skipping up to the porch. "It's good luck!"

"It's a custom that both our countries share," Nick added.

"It's so romantic!" Anya sighed, leaning against the banister.

Toria felt a stab of concern at the girl's raw happiness. It was one thing for Anya to enjoy the impromptu wedding reception at the college. It was another thing for her to take so much delight from the everyday life of the marriage itself.

If that marriage was a sham.

Toria wondered if she hadn't fully thought through the effect on Anya of welcoming the two Sankovitches into her home. Of course, she knew they had to live together in order to make the fiction of man and wife believable. But was it fair to Anya to let her believe they were in love? Or was it fairer to let Anya in on the truth—and force her to lie to the world just as Nick and Toria were lying?

She looked into Anya's, and then Nick's, expectant eyes.

"You're absolutely right," she said, thinking of the promise she had made to do everything in her power to help Anya and Nick stay in the country. "It's a wonderful tradition."

Nick approached her tentatively, his hands large and clumsy as he touched her delicate body.

He had sensed a reluctance to engage in the simple and harmless custom, but he couldn't place her hesitation. For his part, he had known this moment would come and he anticipated many others like it. Moments when they had to act like newlyweds. Moments when they had to appear one way and know in their hearts it was not the truth.

He had made sure to tell his schedule to his secretary that morning, though he seldom shared his plans with her, purely because he knew that she was the type of woman who could not pass up an opportunity to throw a party.

After getting the morning's soil samples from the muddy DuPage River bed, he had picked wildflowers for Toria's bouquet, waxing on and on about love as his research assistants stared openmouthed and dumbfounded. Ha! Professor Sankovitch talking about eternal love and Professor Tryon's beauty. If he weren't so worried about the INS, he would have enjoyed their reaction.

And he had anticipated carrying Toria across the threshold and had thought through the next few days, walking on campus hand in hand, stopping for kisses in places they'd be sure to be seen, his arm lingering possessively around her slender waist...

He had envisioned this marriage and its implications through the restless night before—even anticipating how she would not guess all the deceit that would be required. All because she wasn't the kind of person who ordinarily deceived. Not that he was—but he suspected he had a better idea than she of the hardships and moral dilemmas one faced in the struggle to survive.

He realized that his biggest fear was that she would abruptly give up, deciding that he and his daughter were not worth her trouble—leaving him to scramble for cover from the wrath of the INS, to explain to his daughter, and ponder what it was about himself that made him unworthy of her real attentions, that would always make her out of his reach.

So, as he slipped her crammed briefcase from her hand, he wondered again if he could go through with this and if he had the strength to carry Toria through it when, and if, she faltered. Could he playact sacred vows, quiet Toria's reservations while never giving in to his own, and then, at the right moment, relinquish her without a backward glance so that she could go on with her life?

She was a beautiful and gently cultured woman, he thought. As unattainable in ordinary circumstances as Julia Roberts. And for the moment, she was willing to help him, to playact almost every fantasy he would have about a life with her. He touched the small of her back, the delicate fabric of her blouse like gossamer.

His pride wanted to tell Toria no, don't bother, don't stoop to help if you can't mean it. But his determination to protect his daughter from the instability of his mother country kept his emotions in check.

You have faced more difficult things than a woman, he told himself. Although, as he looked into Toria's eyes—eyes a man could get lost in—he couldn't remember what those difficult things were.

He glanced once at Anya's rapt face and then drew Toria up into his arms. Light as a feather.

Anya pushed open the door and skipped inside to the butter yellow hallway.

"This is so beautiful!" she exclaimed, racing from room to room. "It's a home! A real home! Look, Daddy, look!"

Nick let Toria slip from his arms, and he noted that as if he were distasteful, she disappeared into through a doorway that led to the kitchen.

"Toria, is marriage to me truly awful?" he asked, but she didn't hear him. Or perhaps chose not to.

He looked around the hallway, to the spacious but cozy living room and the airy dining room where an embroidered tablecloth and three place settings had been laid.

"Anya, you're right, it's a home. And..." He paused, nearly adding *for now* but stopped himself. "And now it is our home."

A real home. There was something that made it more than a house. He didn't ordinarily think about this sort of thing, but he wondered what made it so.

Was it the framed watercolors on the wall above the mantel in the living room? Was it the cut-glass vase full of pink tulips on the coffee table? Was it the soft needlepoint pillows piled on the couch? Or the display of mismatched pottery on the dining-room hutch, the cheerful gingham curtains, the subtle scent of vanilla and rosemary?

Whatever it was reminded him that he might as well have lived in a cave for the past months—for most of his life, come to think of it. The two-bedroom apartment he rented on the edge of town was functional and sparse and completely devoid of the touches that made a person want to stay.

It will be so difficult to leave, he thought with a silent groan. And it is so difficult to see Anya drink from this wondrous cup and know that he must take it away from her someday with words she wouldn't understand.

Amicable divorce.

But you always knew that, a voice within him accused.

"I'm going to get my Barbies from the truck," Anya said. "Toria, where am I going to sleep?"

"Yours is the room with the pink-and-yellow quilt on the bed," Toria called out from the dining room.

Anya ran out the front door.

Nick followed Toria through the swinging door to the kitchen. He sniffed the warm-pastry smell from the oven.

"I'm making quiche and salad," Toria said. She chopped carrots on a cutting board. "I hope that's all right. It might not be the kind of food you're used to."

"It will be wonderful," Nick assured her.

"What will you tell Anya when we break up?" Toria asked abruptly.

"I will tell her that many marriages break up," he said carefully. "And that we are still friends. Always friends. That we are...the American expression... amicable. And one day, when she's old enough, I'll explain everything. She will be as grateful then as I am now."

"Is it fair to her to do it this way? To let her think she's in a permanent home when we both know..." Toria paused as she heard the screech and bang of the wooden screen door opening and then slamming shut. She waited until Anya was upstairs before continuing quietly. "When we both know that this is only a temporary thing?"

She thought she saw him flinch at the word *temporary*.

"It is better than the alternative," he said. "Better than to ask her to lie to everyone—her teacher, her friends, herself."

"The INS wouldn't interview her, though, would they?"

"I don't know," Nick admitted. "But they would certainly interview her teachers and the parents of her friends. Every time we take someone, anyone, into our confidence, we put them at risk. To lie to protect us or to tell the truth. Is that fair?"

"Then I guess you're right," she said, wiping her hands of the last bits of lettuce. "But it will be hard on her."

"The alternatives are harder," Nick said quietly.

"GOOD JOB, Anya," Toria said, wiping her hands on her dish towel after putting the last plate in the cabinet. "We're finished."

Anya's shoulders slumped. "Aren't there any more?" she begged.

Toria shook her head. "We've washed all the dishes. We've put them all away. That's all there is to do."

"It's just…they're so pretty. Your dishes. I like to wash them and touch them."

"They're just odds and ends from my family. Nothing matches. Almost everything has chips. And it's all very old."

"But they're wonderful," Anya protested. "I especially love the blue plates. With the tiny gold flowers."

Toria was puzzled by Anya's fascination with her china. "What do you use at home?"

"We used to use these plastic plates from Crate & Barrel. But now that we're a family, we'll get to use real china every day. Say we can, Toria, every night? Please. I promise to wash them every night. And I won't break a single one."

"All right. You're on. I can hardly refuse somebody who wants to wash dishes. Come with me. I think I have something you might like."

Anya followed Toria to the dining-room pine hutch. Toria opened the glass door and pulled from the top shelf a tray no larger than the palm of her hand. On the tray was a complete tea set: two cups and saucers, a pitcher, creamer and sugar bowl.

Anya's eyes widened.

"I used it when I was a little girl," Toria explained. "Why don't you take this up to your Barbie dolls?"

"Wow! Can I keep them for always?"

Toria opened her mouth to say yes.

"Anya," Nick's gruff voice warned from the living room. Toria hadn't even been aware that he was around, he had disappeared so quickly after dinner.

"Sorry," Anya said. "I didn't mean to ask."

"Don't be," Toria said. "You can have them. For always."

She looked significantly across the hallway to Nick. He quelled his prideful admonition.

"Oh, thank you!" Anya cried. "I'll be very careful with them."

She gingerly took the tray from Toria's hand and, in slow motion, walked up the stairs.

"You didn't need to do that," Nick said quietly.

Toria crossed the hall into the living room. He had pulled an armchair up to the other side of her desk and was writing on the back of what looked to be interoffice memo paper. The furniture seemed undersize for him, or perhaps he was too large a man for the house. In any event, he didn't look comfortable.

"I know I don't need to do it," Toria said. "But I like her very much. That's why I'm here now, right?"

"But isn't that . . . tea set, isn't it the sort of thing a woman wants to hand down to her own daughter?"

Toria felt her heart leap into her throat. How could she explain to him that she already thought of Anya as . . . a daughter?

"It's just a little something that my parents gave me long ago," she said, taking the chair across from him.

"You have already been extraordinarily generous with me and my daughter."

"It's just a tea set," Toria said, a little more forcefully than she had meant.

"Don't give her, or me, anything that you'll regret later," he said, his eyes piercing hers.

Toria was the first to look away. Nick returned to finishing his memo.

"I already have," she whispered, thinking of how much she loved Anya. How much her heart would ache when she left. Even how much she had felt moved by the ceremony. What would she feel like as a divorcée?

"What did you say?" he asked, as he put a careful flourish at the end of a sentence he was writing.

"Nothing," she said, pulling her briefcase from the floor beside her chair. "I'm going to try to finish grading these exams. The registrar's office has been leaving frantic messages demanding to know why I haven't finished them."

Nick's hand shot out and grabbed her wrist. Though his grip was gentle, the force behind it was unmistakable.

He shook his head. "Not tonight," he said.

Toria shivered, though Nick had laid a roaring fire in the fireplace. "What do you mean—not tonight?" she asked.

"Tonight, we have a lot of things to do together," he said. "I'm sure the registrar's office will understand—this is our wedding night and you need to spend it with your new husband."

Chapter Eight

"What kind of things are we going to do?" Toria asked, as scandalous images flashed through her mind. Her mouth went dry. She wondered how much she'd actually protest against...

"Do you have your appointment book?"

Puzzled, she pulled the black-canvas date book from her briefcase. He took it from her and leafed through its pages.

"Ah, yes, just what I thought," he said, finger poised on the scribbled mess she had made of July.

"What?"

"You went to the conference on English as a second language...in the second week of July...at the University of Minnesota."

"So?"

"So, here is what I've been working on since dinner."

He turned the page around so that she could read it. As she did, she felt a bright blush spread all over her face. All over her body. If the page had burst into flames from the white-hot intensity of its prose, she wouldn't have been surprised.

"It's a love letter," Nick explained matter-of-factly. "I'm calculating we had sex on our third date. So, at the time of this love letter, we would have had sex maybe...let me think...on at least six occasions, and I would have missed you terribly while you were away at the conference."

"Sex on our third date?" Toria asked hollowly, pushing the paper back across the desk.

"I read an article in *Sophisticated Woman* magazine that advised women that the best time to have sex is on the third date," Nick elaborated. "It's called the Third-Date Rule. Earlier than that, and he thinks you're loose. Later, and he loses interest."

"You read this?"

"I borrowed it this morning from my secretary's office before my fieldwork," he admitted. "I was attracted by the cover article on 'How to Get Him to the Altar.' I thought it might give us some tips on explaining how we made the decision to marry."

"And then you ended up reading about this Third-Date Rule?"

He nodded. "I also ordered something from the back pages."

"Oh, Nick! That's ridiculous."

"You need a . . . what did they call it? A trousseau. It'll all come UPS in about a week."

"What did you get?"

"The usual bride's stuff," Nick shrugged. "A white robe and a matching gown," he said with a groan.

Toria looked heavenward. She could just imagine.

"I'm not that kind of woman," she pointed out. "I don't wear the sort of stuff that would make a man, would make you, groan like that."

"I didn't mean any offense," he said. "I just wanted to have the purchase to show up on my credit-card bill. You don't even have to open the package when it comes. Although maybe you should. Just so you know what it looks like."

He took out his pen. "What do you wear to bed normally, on an average night?"

"Why do you need to know?"

"I think it should be pretty obvious why."

"Cotton," Toria nearly spat the word.

"Cotton what?"

"Cotton everything," she said, throwing up her arms.

He looked at her, ready to ask for specifics. But the look on her face told him No, don't ask, or expect to get a slap in the face, buddy.

"Why don't we just move on?" he suggested.

"Do you make love on the third date?" Toria asked crisply, taking the offensive.

"I haven't gone on a date in so long that I don't remember."

"Why not? You've got something of a following at the college."

"I wasn't aware."

"You'd have to be brain-dead to not notice. You practically have a fan club. You mean to tell me that none of the coeds have approached you?"

"I would think of it as a breach of ethics to date a student. So I have always declined. No matter how...forward their suggestions."

"Well, how about faculty women?"

Nick felt his face go red-hot. "Professors have made themselves clear," he said. "But I haven't responded."

She looked oddly pleased by this—and then he noticed she seemed instantly flustered by her own delight.

"So why no dates?" she persisted.

"Simple. Anya. I haven't found somebody who thinks a nice date is taking Anya and her friend Becky out for pizza and a movie. A G-rated movie, something by Disney. Then maybe a little shopping at a toy store."

"I think that would sound okay."

He studied her. "Maybe we were made for each other," he mused. "Just for the purposes of the INS, you understand."

"Sure. But if a woman were willing to go out for these romantic dates with two eight-year-old chaperones, would you honestly lose interest if she didn't make love to you by the third date?"

He shook his head and thought to himself, *I never even got a first date with you, Toria, and my interest in you was always constant—longings and desires that I have for so long squelched. I would have "dated" you forever.*

"I don't normally read American women's magazines," he confessed. "I hadn't even heard of this third-date American custom before. And besides, we don't really even have 'dating' in Byleukrainia. Marriages are arranged."

"Well, I don't have sex on the third date and this 'rule' doesn't really qualify as an American custom. I'm not sure too many women would know what you're talking about."

He looked up from her appointment book. "Then when do you do it?"

Toria opened her mouth, closed it, looked into the fire, then stared at Nick with outright indignation.

"I don't have a scientific system for deciding, and there's no universally accepted American tradition," she said, her chin jutting out ever so slightly. "But the few times it's happened with me, it's been when I've been...in a committed relationship based on love and caring."

Nick stared at her impassively.

"It's none of your business," Toria snapped. "How many times that's happened is ancient history."

"And when the INS talks to us, I have to be a pretty good historian about the life of my bride," Nick insisted. "I'm sorry. It shouldn't be. But when we have to defend our marriage, we'd better know everything."

The grandfather clock tolled eight times. The fire crackled and hissed. From upstairs, they heard Anya's giggles as she instructed a Barbie doll on proper tea-party etiquette.

"There was one guy in college," Toria said at last. "And one man after graduate school."

"How long?"

"How long what?"

"How long before you slept with them? How long did the relationships last? How long in between?"

"A long time, in each case, before we...had sex. In both cases. I, well, I thought we were committed to each other, to a future together. I had known Jack—the boy from college—all my life and we started dating when I was a freshman. We made love..." She stumbled over the words as if she were eating peanut butter.

"Take your time," Nick said soothingly. "Breathe deeply. And try again."

Toria took a breath, but she felt as if she were sucking fire through a straw. These were private memories she hadn't even shared with any of her closest girlfriends. Not even Missy. Maybe especially not Missy, come to think of it. Missy would giggle too much.

"We made love sometime in my sophomore year, and we broke up when we were seniors. The other man, Laurence, was a romance-languages professor at University of Illinois, where I got my degree. We slept together after six months of dating. We were engaged at that point. The relationship lasted two or three months after that. We obviously didn't get married."

She met his openmouthed gaze with a challenging stare.

"So you slept with your college boyfriend after a year of dating and the other man after six months?" Nick asked.

"Correct."

"And there have been no other men?"

"No," she said. "Nick , I don't like being interrogated this way."

"I don't like doing the interrogating. But I have to. By the way, we won't have time for your morals."

"What do you mean?"

"We met in June, at the dean's party. We're married in September. We had to have...gotten together much earlier than you're used to. I say three dates."

"*Sophisticated Woman* is not how every woman is."

"You think my secretary is a little fast?"

Toria smiled in spite of herself, thinking of the sixtyish woman she had met at the party.

"It's a fun magazine," she admitted. "I even read it when I'm at the dentist. But don't think that any magazine is a guide to how I act."

"So when did you sleep with me? Theoretically, of course."

"I guess whenever we fell in love."

"And it took you a year to fall in love with your first boyfriend?"

"I thought I was in love," Toria said. "I felt...comfortable with Jack. I thought I would be with Jack the rest of my life. I didn't...I didn't exactly fall in love, I just loved him. I still do, just not in that way. I'm his daughter's godmother—I even set him up on a blind date with his wife. And, as for Laurence, the...other man, I thought we had a future together." She left out that part of her attraction to Laurence had been a fear that life was passing her by. That if she didn't start experiencing more and dreaming less, she would regret it later. When she was older . . . and alone.

Nick's eyebrows drew together.

"So, if you were to fall in love with the man you were meant to be with for the rest of your life, how long would it take you to know?"

"I don't know. Maybe it would happen at first sight. Maybe it would take a few weeks. Maybe it would take a few years."

"But it could theoretically happen on the first date."

"Yes."

"And if he felt the same way, you'd both know on the first date that you were in love."

"I suppose," Toria agreed cautiously.

"So you could make love as early as the first date if it were with the right man," he concluded. "Maybe even as early as the night of the dean's party."

Toria felt cornered. "All right," she conceded. "It's theoretically possible. But it wouldn't have happened. That isn't the kind of woman I am. I've never had a one-night stand and I've never had a love-at-first-sight experience. I've been cautious, really cautious, in love. I've thought, sometimes, that somebody I'm dating might turn out to be someone I could love, but something's always stopped me from . . ." She felt limp under Nick's heavy-lidded stare. "What about you? I mean, we're focusing on how long it would take me to make love with you. How long would it take you to get to know a woman before you made love to her?"

Nick smiled lazily.

"With the right woman, it would take only an instant to decide. And the loving would take me all night."

Toria looked away, embarrassed.

"Is that how you are all the time or are you just baiting me?"

"No, I'm not baiting you. I've never had the experience of a one-night stand," he admitted. "I met Anya's mother when her family was fleeing the fighting in our capital. They were refugees and my family took them in. Ordinarily, our culture is so conservative that a woman would never give herself to a man outside of marriage. But the times were unstable. She was determined to have experiences.... I think she knew, deep in her heart, that she was not fated to have a long life. When she left with her family, as they fled the fighting, my heart was broken. I never knew she was pregnant. When she died in shelling two years later, her family brought Anya to me. Anya was a burden to them. But never to me. I always wanted her, from the moment I found her on my doorstep."

Toria gasped. "They just left her there?"

"Anya was born outside of marriage. In our country, that was a terrible thing. I don't know how her mother managed to keep her, but once she was dead, Anya's grandparents did not consider her a part of their family."

"So Anya doesn't know her mother or her mother's family."

"No, she doesn't remember. And as for romance since then, there have been ... some women. Not many, but a few."

"And did you love any of them?" Toria asked softly.

"No, but that wasn't a condition of our coming together. I didn't love them, they didn't love me—or at least no one said she loved me and I never made any promises. But that is over now. I have to think of Anya first. I can't have affairs, can't have a revolving door for women. Besides, even if I fell in love, I'm not even sure I'd know how to tell a woman."

"Just say the words," Toria suggested.

Nick smiled and then looked away. "First date," he said abruptly.

"Sixth date," Toria countered.

"Third."

"Fifth."

He crumbled up the love note and threw it into the fire.

He opened the date book and searched the pages.

"Fourth date. My final offer. After the graduation reception," he announced. "We had a few glasses of champagne on the quad lawn and slipped upstairs to your office."

Toria shook her head.

"My office? That just sounds too...risqué," she said. "We would have gone back to my house."

"Oh, but Professor Tryon, I mean, my darling, risqué is just what you're looking for. Why else would you marry a man like me?"

A HALF HOUR LATER, he had used up sixteen sheets of interoffice memo paper, four pieces of yellow message pad, and one North Central College letter-head.

Toria had stagnated at exam number seventeen. As she struggled to keep her mind on her work, she ended up watching, fascinated, as he combed through her date book and then compared it with his own.

He looked up and smiled as he caught her watching him.

"Did you go to the English department's Fourth of July picnic at the Riverwalk this year?" he asked.

She shook her head.

"I was home sick with strep throat," she said. "I watched the fireworks from my window."

"Aaaahhh," he said. He rechecked his date book. "Which window?"

"My bedroom," she said. "It's the only one that you can see the Riverwalk from."

"Only from your bedroom? That's perfect," he said, and scribbled on a piece of blank paper with intense concentration.

"Where did you and Anya go for Fourth of July?" Toria asked conversationally.

"It just so happens that Anya had been invited to Becky's house for a sleep-over that night," Nick said. "And me? I spent the night here, watching the fireworks from your bed. We didn't get much sleep. How 'bout we ate fried chicken? That sounds very American. And watermelon. It dripped down your neck, down between . . ."

He bent over to finish his writing.

"Did we have a good time?" Toria asked.

He looked up for an instant, thinking he had offended her with his intimate remark. *My Lord,* he thought, *she has no idea how intimate we will have to be with each other.* But he saw the flicker of amusement and challenge in her eyes and he relaxed.

"We had a very, very good time," he said with a suggestive smile. "All that champagne, fried chicken and blueberry pie does something to a woman."

"To say nothing of the fireworks."

He delighted in the delicate pink blush of her cheeks.

"Could I have a cup of coffee please?" he asked.

"Sure. What do you take?"

"What do you take?"

"I use cream and sugar," Toria said. "But I don't drink coffee at night because it keeps me up."

"I'll have to remember that," Nick said. "Anyhow, I'll have coffee with cream and sugar. And a Coke, too, if it's not too much trouble."

"You want the Coke mixed with the coffee?"

He looked at her blankly. "No, why would I ever mix Coke and coffee?"

She fixed a tray with a cup of coffee, cream with sugar, and placed next to it a glass of Coke. When she returned, he had cleared the desk and had spread the notes on the desk facing her chair. He shook the cup and saucer until a few drops dribbled over the edge of the saucer.

"Watch it!" Toria cried out, as he put the saucer down on top of one of the notes he had spent so much time writing.

Ignoring her, he picked up the saucer, admired the wet coffee ring on the paper and repeated the process on a different note. When he was finished, he blew on the circles to dry them. Then he put the cup and saucer on the tray and proceeded to fold up every note. And then unfolded and refolded every note, until all his hard work looked like yesterday's discarded mail.

Toria stared, sitting on an armchair with her head propped up on her fists. "What are you doing?"

"You'll see," he said mysteriously.

At last, he leaned back in his chair, popped open his soda and smiled proudly at the mess he had laid out in front of him.

"Here are my declarations of love," he said. "You have read them over so many times. Now it's your turn to write back."

Chapter Nine

My darling Victoria,
The late-summer roses bloom, opening their petals to the morning sun—filling the air with your scent stolen from your body. With every heartbeat, I long for you. I will come to your office at one. Leave the door open and wait at the couch by the window. I can see now in my mind's eye the golden light upon your hair. That vision will sustain me until tomorrow.

Love,
Nicky

Dearest,
When the first leaves change, I dream of seasons to come. I hope all of them I share with you—the bright, stark light of winter's snow, the fresh green spring, the scorching summer. Spend all those days with me. Marry me.

Yours forever,
Nicky

Toria put the paper back down on the desk and swallowed. Before her was an array of love notes—

some were just hurried notes confirming dates, others had more depth, some were very explicit. All would be deeply moving, even suggestive if there was any truth to them.

"Don't you think this is a little explicit?" she asked, pointing to one.

My darling Victoria,
When you cried out, I thought that I had hurt you. The thought was torment. And yet, I had mistook that sound—you said you were surprised at the feel of me inside you. Oh, tender one, when I enter you...

"I have to write like a man in love," Nick said with a shrug.

"You would write a letter like this?"

"If I were in love. At least I think so. I've never been in love," he admitted, looking away uncomfortably. "I felt deeply for Anya's mother—still do, for the part of her that lives on in Anya. But falling in love with the kind of passion that would lead to marriage, I can only guess at."

"But you're so explicit!"

"I know I would give myself completely to my woman. And I would feel no shame about speaking or writing about all my feelings. Even the ones that are sexual. Especially the ones that are sexual. I don't separate the sexual side of myself from all others—even if I don't date."

"But won't you feel funny about such personal stuff being used to prove something to the INS?"

"I wish it were not so," Nick said cautiously. "But the words, they are harmless because they are..."

"Make-believe," Toria supplied.

"And please remember—I don't mean to be offensive to your sensibilities."

"I know."

"But now can you write back? As a woman in love."

Toria recoiled.

"You don't need to be so explicit if that is not your nature," Nick said quickly.

Toria fingered the worn letter.

"Do we really need this? Wouldn't just exchanging our life stories do as well? If I knew your mother's maiden name? If you knew whether I like my eggs scrambled or fried? Won't that be enough?"

"No, that wouldn't be enough," Nick said. "You forget. Byleukrainia wants me back for arms research and to be a leader. The country is in turmoil. There are many of my compatriots who want to come here to America. The INS will be doing its job with the Byleukrainian government and every refugee looking over its shoulder. The INS will be especially vigilant for deceit."

"I've never written love letters," Toria said.

Nick prodded the dying embers of the fire with a poker.

"It's late," he said gently. "Do it tomorrow. It's a lot to think about. And we have so much other stuff to work on."

"Like what?"

His eyes met hers.

"Like whether you like your eggs scrambled or fried."

Anya appeared at the living-room door, dressed in a white flannel nightgown and purple bunny slippers. Of course it wouldn't be Anya without the imprint of grape-juice drops, which had faded but not disappeared with repeated washing.

"It's almost time for *Bewitched*," she said.

Nick looked at his watch.

"You're right," he said. "I'll run out to the truck and get the TV."

"You brought a television?" Toria exclaimed.

"We knew you didn't have one."

"How come you don't?" Anya asked. "How can you live without it?"

Toria sighed, trying to figure out how best to explain.

"My parents thought that television was destroying our culture," she said. "They were academics— my father was even dean of the school for a while. They were both very interested in preserving what is important in our culture. They thought it was better to spend an evening reading or listening to classical music than watching television."

"In America, everyone is free to live their own life when they turn twenty-one," Nick said. "Why didn't you buy one then?"

"My parents were very frail but still determined to live in this house instead of going to a nursing home. I took care of them until last year, and I knew that buying a television set would upset them too much. Kind of like if I announced I was taking them to a rock concert or if I dyed my hair pink.''

"And then they died?'' Anya asked. "You must miss them very much.''

"I do miss them. They died within a few weeks of each other,'' Toria said, thinking back to the last, difficult months. "But for both of them, there was a blessing at the end.''

"Why didn't you buy a television set afterward?'' Anya persisted.

"I guess it never occurred to me,'' Toria admitted.

Nick studied her carefully. "You were very dutiful,'' he said. "So very dutiful.''

Toria shook her head. "They were my parents. Any daughter would do the same.''

"Didn't it get in the way of living your own life?''

Toria pressed her lips together. "Absolutely not,'' she said vehemently. "That was my life.''

Nick shrugged. "Well, now we're your life,'' he said, putting his arm around Anya. "I have a feeling that things are going to be shook up a little. Television's just the beginning. After tonight, I think we'll have to introduce you to the music of the Rolling Stones and the films of Schwarzenegger.''

LATER, TORIA SAT at her dressing table and pulled the tortoiseshell pins from her hair. She hummed a lilting tune, and then stopped self-consciously as she realized it was the theme music from *Bewitched*.

So what's wrong with that? she chided herself.

Her life could use a little shaking up. She didn't always have to hum Chopin or Beethoven or Verdi.

Her chestnut hair uncoiled and fell in soft waves against her washed-cotton robe. As she absently brushed her hair, her eyes met their reflection in the mirror. She tried to twitch her lips the way that Elizabeth Montgomery did. It was kind of fun. Then she looked closer.

Did she really have "amber-flamed" eyes? she wondered, her cheeks flushing lightly at the memory of Nick's manufactured love letter. Did her eyes really glow with an inner fire?

She had never thought much about the color of her eyes. When asked by the Illinois Department of Motor Vehicles, she had checked brown. Her only other choices had been black, blue, hazel and green. There hadn't been a space for amber. Or inner fires.

She leaned even closer.

There were flecks of gold shot through the brown, and this could certainly be verified by any INS bureaucrat. Thank goodness Nick was keeping his facts straight.

But also how intriguing that he noticed things about herself that had always gone unnoticed. Did others think of her when they smelled a rose? she wondered, holding her palm up to her nose. Had anyone ever admired the freckles on her nose? Had anyone ever thought the tiny mole at the side of her mouth was sexy? Would she cry out softly if he . . .

She abruptly dropped the brush on the vanity and walked out into the hallway. It was unnerving to be

the object of passion, even if the passion was manufactured.

The door to the bathroom was open, and inside,
Nick counted as Anya brushed her teeth.

"Are you finding everything all right?" Toria
asked.

"Twenty-six, twenty-seven, twenty-eight," Nick
continued steadily. "Twenty-nine, thirty. All right,
Anya, you're finished."

Anya spat out her toothpaste in the sink. Nick
turned on the water and washed away the foam.

"This house is great," Anya said, her mouth dripping greenish white. "I really like it here. I especially
like my room. It's how a princess would live."

Toria laughed. "It's just some old wicker furniture that my parents got from their parents. I think
princesses sleep on velvet and gold."

Anya shook her head solemnly. "Real princesses
sleep on wicker and linen and pretty quilts."

Nick rinsed off the toothbrush. "Now it's time to
brush your hair," he said.

Anya looked stricken. "I think I forgot to pack my
brush!"

"Go on into my room and find one on the vanity," Toria suggested.

Anya crossed the hall and let out a shriek. "Now
this is how princesses really do it!" she cried.

Nick smiled at Toria. "She thinks you're the most
wonderful woman in the world," he said.

"And I think she's the most wonderful little girl."

Anya came back with Toria's silver-backed brush.
"Can I really use this?"

"You can," Toria reassured her.

"It's really beautiful."

"It was my mother's."

"You have a lot of old, beautiful things in your house," Anya observed. "Can I use some lotion from the crystal bottle?"

"Sure, let me help you open it," Toria said.

They walked back to Toria's room and Anya sat down on the embroidered vanity stool.

Nick stuck his head in the doorway. "I'm going to get the rest of the stuff out of the truck," he said. "All right if I take the other bedroom?"

"Yes, of course. I set it up for you. There's guest towels and a robe on the bed." She mentally checked off the other things she had laid out for his use—a tray of fruit, a carafe of water with a matching glass and several news magazines for late-night reading.

Toria turned back to look at Anya's reflection in the mirror. "Here's the hand lotion—"

Anya, beet red to the roots of her hair, burst into sobs.

"Anya, sweet pea, what's the matter?" Toria asked, putting her arms around the stricken girl.

Anya sobbed and gulped, sobbed and gulped. "You're getting a divorce!" she exclaimed into the folds of Toria's robe. "You don't really love each other!"

Toria didn't know what to say. It was true that one day they would get a divorce. Had Anya figured out the truth?

She stooped down to cradle the weeping girl and waited for Nick to come back. She hoped he would know how to explain everything to his daughter. It seemed to take forever, but at last, Nick's strong footsteps came up the stairs. He appeared at the doorway, a garment bag flung over his shoulders.

"What's the matter?" he asked, putting down his load.

Anya pulled out of Toria's embrace and stared at her father with a mixture of grief and anger. "You're not even married for a whole day and you're getting ready for a divorce," she accused.

"What are you talking about?" Nick demanded.

"Separate bedrooms." Anya paused to let her words sink in. "That's the first sign."

"First sign of what?" Toria asked.

"Divorce!" Anya sobbed. "Jeremy Smith's parents started sleeping in separate bedrooms and they were divorced only two months later. He told me. It's the first sign of it. Next you'll be asking me to ask the other one to pass the salt. Then you'll be dividing your CDs."

"I can already guess where Van Halen's going," Nick quipped.

Toria shushed him with an angry look. This was serious! She remembered Anya had brought daily reports to her office about how Jeremy Smith's parents' divorce had rocked the second-grade classroom.

"Anya, not everything turns out like it did in Jeremy's family."

"But don't you want to sleep together?"

Silence. Uncomfortable silence. Very uncomfortable silence.

"Some people prefer separate bedrooms," Toria said at last.

"But not people who love each other," Anya shot back. "It's pretty weird, if you ask me. Makes me think you don't love each other as much as you should."

Toria's mind raced as she considered the implications of Anya's position. She came to a quick decision. She'd deal with the consequences later.

"Anya, you didn't let me finish," she said. "As I was saying, some people prefer separate bedrooms and you shouldn't make judgments about them. But we aren't going to be sleeping in separate bedrooms."

"We aren't?" Nick choked out.

"Of course not, darling," Toria said sweetly. "I thought we agreed you would use the other room for storing your clothes and books. There isn't enough closet space in here."

Nick looked at the bed, a strictly feminine confection of lace-covered pillows, delicate floral sheets and pink wedding-ring quilt. He swallowed hard.

"And we were thinking about closet space," Toria continued. "Weren't we, darling?"

As Nick looked around the feminine lair, the last thing on his mind was closet space. But he nodded.

"Now, Anya, it's time to say good-night," Toria said. "You've got school tomorrow. Today was a special day off only."

Anya reached out to give her father a hug.

"Good night," she said. "But tell me if you guys ever fall out of love. You two deserve happiness. And I deserve a home."

Overcome with emotion, Toria hugged Anya tightly. Nick leaned over and kissed his daughter on the top of her head, leaving behind the subtle scent of lime.

A home—this deception wouldn't give Anya the home she was expecting, but would give her the stable life she—that every child—deserved.

But as she hugged Anya tighter, Toria realized that she was not being completely unselfish. It felt good to have Anya here. It felt good to have Nick here—even if his made-up love letters embarrassed her. She hadn't known how quiet her house had been until these two had brought their television and their talk, their boisterousness and their enthusiasm. She hadn't known how quiet her own life had been.

She kissed the top of Anya's hair.

"I love you so much," Anya said. "Can I . . . can I call you Mom?"

Toria felt a mixture of delight and guilt. She looked up at Nick. She could see the war within him.

"She doesn't remember much about her own mother," he reminded Toria. "It would be all right with me, if it's all right with you."

Anya tugged at Toria.

"Can I?" she asked again.

Toria took a deep breath.

"Yes, that would be all right," she said cautiously. "Mom is just fine."

Anya squealed with happiness. Then, after much parental cajoling about the need for a good night's sleep before school, she skipped off to her room— leaving the two adults to warily regard each other from either side of the conjugal bed.

Chapter Ten

"I'll go downstairs and watch the news," Nick said. "I always do."

"Even on your wedding night?" Toria teased.

His eyes registered mild surprise and then a kind of appraisal that made Toria pull modestly at the lapels of her robe and step back behind the protection of a wicker stool.

"If you'd like me to stay..." he suggested, gesturing to the bed.

"No, of course not," she said hastily. "I was just making a joke."

"A joke," he repeated.

"Yes, a joke."

He crossed to the door. "You were just saying all that to Anya to..."

"Yes, just for her sake," Toria said.

"And what you just said now was a joke."

"I told you it was a joke," she insisted.

His slight smile mocked her seriousness.

"Good night, Nick," she said. She tightened the belt on her robe and fussed with some books on the nightstand.

"Then I'll just watch Letterman until Anya goes to sleep," he said. He paused at the door and looked back at her.

"And after that, you'll...?" Toria asked.

"I'll go to sleep in the guest room. If that's what you want."

Toria nodded briskly, satisfied. "What time does she wake up?"

"Six-thirty."

"Then we'd better be up before she is."

"I'll set my alarm," he said stiffly. "Are you going to sleep now?"

"Yes, it's been a very long day."

"Then good night. I wish that I knew words that could express my gratitude, but all I have is thank you."

"Don't thank me until you get your visa."

He smiled ruefully. "If, Toria. If."

David Letterman's guest was a blonde, stitched into a red dress that was so bright that it vibrated on the screen. Or maybe that was her body vibrating.

She was the star of some new sitcom. Nothing worse than some empty-headed celebrity you've never heard of gushing on and on about how fame hasn't changed them, Nick thought.

He switched off the TV and checked his watch. Ten forty-five. If Anya wasn't asleep by now, he'd be very surprised. She had had a long and exciting day.

He crept upstairs, keeping his footsteps light so as not to wake anyone. Living a life on the run had taught him how to walk through a forest, through a street, without making a sound. But he hadn't counted on the creak! of oak floors in a hundred-year-old farmhouse.

"Daddy?" Anya asked, appearing in the dark hallway.

Caught!

"Sweetie, you must be exhausted. And you have school tomorrow. You have to go to sleep."

"Something wrong?" Toria asked, coming out of her room to stand beside Anya.

"You can't sleep, either?" Nick asked.

"Truthfully, no. I'm just a little...I don't know. A little wired."

"You've never had a wedding night before," Anya pointed out. "In our old country, the wedding party lasts for a week. Nobody has a bedtime," she concluded, with enough of a pout that it was clear which country she believed to have better wedding customs.

"What do you know about wedding parties?" Nick asked.

"You told me."

"But this is America and we do things differently," Toria pointed out. "You have school tomorrow. I do, too. I have to teach a class at eight."

"Well, I know exactly how to put everybody to sleep," Nick said confidently.

"You do?" Toria asked.

"Yeah. Get your clothes on," he ordered Toria.

"Me too?" Anya cried.

"You can leave on your pj's. But put on your robe."

"What are we doing?" Toria asked.

"We're going to the most wonderful place on earth," Nick said mysteriously.

"I'LL TAKE a Big Mac, large fries and a medium Diet Coke," Nick said. He looked down at Anya. "What do you want?"

"Chocolate milk shake."

"Did you eat all of your dinner?" he asked with mock severity.

Anya nodded. "Every bite," she confirmed.

"Okay, then you can have a milk shake."

He communicated the order and then looked at Toria.

"I don't want anything," she said.

"Make that two chocolate milk shakes," Nick said into the speaker. "And throw in an extra order of fries."

"You know, we just fit," Anya said to Toria as Nick eased the pickup to the cash-register window. "I like that."

"What do you mean?" Toria asked.

"When me and Dad drive around at night, I have to bring a pillow or I can't get comfortable. But now we have you."

Anya snuggled up to Toria, who put her arms around the little girl.

"Isn't this nice?" Anya asked. "You're so much better than a pillow."

Toria kissed the top of Anya's head.

"Yes, it is nice," she agreed.

"But you don't completely approve," Nick pointed out.

"I think it's a little unorthodox," Toria said, choosing her words carefully. She watched Anya take a giant slurp of her chocolate shake, thinking it would be a far better thing for the girl to be in bed.

"You don't go out late, do you?" Nick asked.

"No," Toria admitted. "Especially not on weeknights."

"And you don't go to McDonald's much."

"I haven't been since...I don't remember when."

"How come?"

Toria thought about it while Nick handed out the food and selected an out-of-the-way parking place. The harvest moon blinked through the canopy of trees.

"I guess because I spent a lot of time taking care of my parents," Toria explained. "They needed a pretty consistent schedule, especially as it became harder for them to do things. We always had lunch at twelve-thirty. Afternoon tea at four. Reading in the study until dinnertime. Music in the living room until ten o'clock. And I arranged my teaching schedule and my work on my degree around that."

"You could have reserved the nights for yourself," Nick pointed out.

Toria shook her head. "Going out late at night wasn't something I could do—not that they discouraged me. It's just there never was enough time, or maybe I wasn't sufficiently interested. Even though they've been gone for more than a year, I haven't changed much."

"You really were a good daughter," Nick remarked. "Were they proud of you when you came to teach at the same college they had?"

Toria smiled. "They were a little disappointed, I think, that I didn't do something more academic. Teaching reading and English to incoming freshmen—so much of it remedial—wasn't what they would have liked."

"But you teach something useful," Nick noted.

"Very useful. I don't like all these eggheads who write papers and more papers on things that won't do anybody any good."

"Do you think what you do is going to do somebody good?"

"Of course it will. I'd like to figure out a way to help this little patch of the planet stay clean and do it in a way that won't take away any jobs. And on top of that, I try to show a few college kids how they leave the earth. It's like teaching them to clean their room but on a slightly grander scale."

"So how do you justify this?" she asked impishly, pointing to his nearly finished sandwich.

"Balance, Toria, balance. In every life, there must be balance," he said. "What were you expecting? For me to eat bean sprouts and tofu?"

"Before I knew you, yes."

"Don't worry. I eat like that a lot of the time. But I don't deny myself these simple pleasures. Simple pleasures are what make life worth living."

He finished his sandwich and started the car.

"Let's go for a ride," he said. "How about Iowa?"

"Yeah! Yeah!" Anya exclaimed.

"Iowa's nearly two hundred miles away," Toria said.

"You disapprove?"

"You bet I do! It's late. She should be in bed. She has school tomorrow. I should be home, too. I have an eight o'clock class."

"In your country, you have a custom. A honeymoon, yes?"

Toria nodded.

"Well, we'll drive to Iowa and back before morning. That will be our honeymoon."

He pulled out onto the nearly deserted Plank Road.

"Sometimes we drive all night," Anya explained. "To Kentucky. To Indiana. Once we went all the way to Michigan. And then we got home just before it was time for me to go to school."

Anya put her arms around Toria, resting her head on her shoulder.

"Nick, this is wrong!" Toria cried out, truly shocked at his behavior. "It's after eleven. We all have work to do tomorrow. It's unhealthy for a child to stay up this late. I knew with the excitement of the day that she'd have trouble sleeping, but this is wrong."

"Do you really believe we're going all the way to Iowa?" Nick whispered.

"With you, I would believe anything."

He took them down Ogden, turning off at Plank, driving in the quiet darkness.

"Hey, you've missed the exit to the highway," Toria pointed out.

"Exactly," Nick said, pulling up to the winding driveway that led to her house. "And look at Anya."

Toria looked down at the sleeping girl.

"She's dreaming of highways," Nick said. "Dreaming of Iowa—she's never been there, you know."

He got out, came around and slid Anya carefully out of the truck cab. Toria followed him to the house, slipping in front of him to unlock the door. Effortlessly, he took the steps two at a time. Toria followed, and as he stood in Anya's darkened bedroom, she pulled back the sheets and ferreted out a teddy bear from under the bed. Then, with surpassing gentleness, Nick laid his daughter down and tucked her into the sheets.

"She's still on her way to Iowa," he said softly.

They closed the door quietly behind themselves.

"I'm sorry," Toria said.

"For what?"

"For thinking I knew better how to be a parent."

He looked puzzled. "You probably would be a better parent. Nobody's given me a degree in this— I've gotten all my training on the job. Sometimes I wish somebody would point out when I'm doing a less than perfect job. I don't even want to think about the next stages—telephones, curfews, boys."

"You're doing great—you're just a little unconventional," Toria said. "I would never think of putting a kid in a car and driving until she fell asleep. But it worked for Anya."

They lingered underneath the crystal hall light.

"Did the trip to Iowa make you sleepy, too?" he teased.

"It's time for bed, if that's what you're asking."

"Then accept my good-night," he said, and he reached for her hand.

She expected the forthright handshake that might have been awkward but perfectly correct. Instead, he kissed the back of her hand. She shivered at the sensual touch of his warm breath lingering on her skin.

"In my country, long ago," he said, straightening but not relinquishing her hand, "a knight pledged his life and loyalty to the tsarina by kissing her hand. And here—" he turned her hand over and closed her fingers over her palm "—here is where she held the knight's heart. And his fate. With a single word, she could grant him wealth and privilege or banish him or worse. That is how it is with you and me—you hold the key to my future. To help me, you must come to know me more intimately than you have known any other man. And I must be more intimate with you than you have ever experienced."

Toria stepped back, taking her hand away from him as if he were a hot oven. She remembered the moment of their wedding vows, how she had felt united to him even if their arrangement were nothing more than a sham, meant nothing to him other than a means to protect himself and his daughter from deportation.

Now, as his blue eyes bored into her, she shivered. He meant intimacy, closeness that she only now had a glimpse of.

"I thought we agreed no sex," she said more primly than she intended.

She knew that the sex she had once regarded as lovemaking was no match for the kind of no-holds-barred exploration that he would make of her body. He was the kind of man who could break down a woman's every resistance to create a wanton who would exult in both her own surrender and her sensual power over him.

That he was skilled in lovemaking, she had no doubt. Even though she had little experience, she knew from his gentle caress of her hand and the slow burn of his lips against her flesh that he wanted her. She only now appreciated how much. Though it was probable that he only wanted her for the night, for the moment, because of the sheer convenience of her proximity.

She touched the back of her neck, absently checking where her luxuriant hair was cuffed by a wide tortoiseshell barrette.

"I have broken no agreements," Nick protested.

"See that you don't," she said, covering her embarrassment with a feisty tilt of her chin. "Good night, Nick."

"Good night," he said, and then defiantly added, "my wife."

SHE DID EVERYTHING she would ordinarily do to get ready for bed. She changed into a cotton nightgown and matching kimono-style robe. She brushed her hair and unclasped the delicate watch that had been her parents' gift when she graduated from high school.

She felt unsettled, restless, even. She thought about going downstairs for a snack but admitted she wasn't even hungry—the chocolate shake had settled in her stomach like a rock. She considered going downstairs to get her briefcase—maybe she should grade a few more exams—but stopped herself with the realization that she'd have to pass by Nick's door in order to get there.

She stood by the window, looking out at the garden. The moon was full and illuminated each leaf. She even made out the bare outline of a field mouse skipping across the mahogany love seat her father had placed under the arbor.

Then she looked beyond, to the street. A dark blue car was parked near the widow Schank's house. Odd, really, considering that there was a village ordinance forbidding after-midnight parking on the side streets. One of Mrs. Schank's sons must be in from out of town, Toria decided, and he'd just forgotten he'd get a parking ticket by morning.

The breath ran out of her as she realized there was a man sitting in the driver's seat of the car. He looked familiar, but he wasn't one of the Schank brothers. She pulled back the lace curtain and looked more closely.

Her heart started pounding as she realized he was the same man who had stared at her and Nick so intently this afternoon. At the courthouse. Now he sat in his car, occasionally sipping from a foam cup. There appeared to be somebody keeping him company in the passenger's seat, but Toria couldn't make out who.

She felt a chill go through her as she pushed the lace curtain back into place.

"Nick!" she called out. When she didn't hear a response, she ventured out into the hallway. The floorboards creaked—not in their usual comforting way but rather in a new, ominous tone.

She knocked on the guest-room door.

"Nicky," she whispered urgently, not wanting to wake Anya.

Nick opened the door, the bedside reading lamp illuminating his hard body. He wore loose-fitting pajama bottoms of cotton so worn as to be sheer. She gulped. Every muscle on his body was hard and defined, broad at the shoulders and taut at the stomach. His manhood cast a proud, hard silhouette against the straining fabric. As her eyes traveled up to meet his, she saw the suggestive twinkle.

"Yes?" he purred.

"I saw something," she said, knowing her words sounded weak and contrived. "A car parked outside. There is a man in it. I'm sure I saw him this afternoon. At the courthouse."

Sexual invitation cast aside, Nick followed her into her dark room. He leaned toward, but did not disturb, the lace curtains.

"I don't see anything," he said.

"Let me..." Toria came up behind him, standing on tiptoe to see over his shoulder.

The car wasn't there.

"There was a car," Toria protested. "Right there, with a guy—I knew I had seen him this afternoon."

Nick turned around and leaned back against the windowsill. He put his hands on either side of her tiny waist, gathering up the delicate fabric of her robe and dress. Toria bristled at the frankly sexual touch, but was too wrought up to challenge him.

"He was staring at me in the most peculiar way this afternoon, in the hall," she continued. "I didn't say anything at the time because when I looked back at him, he was gone. Nick, I think someone's following us."

"Yes?" he asked quietly, dropping his head forward so that his warm breath caressed the skin where her robe had fallen from her shoulder.

Toria suddenly yanked away from him. Or rather, Nick relinquished her—because he clearly had the muscle and the strength to hold her exactly where he wanted.

"You think I made that up!"

"No," he said, and clearly meant yes.

"You think I invited you in here just to..."

"No, of course not," he soothed, but his tone made it clear he was saying, "I sure did."

"Get out of here, Nick," she ordered, ignoring the rebellious quiver of her thighs.

Nervous about facing him down? You bet, she thought, and that was the explanation for her body's flushed feeling, for her breasts' betrayal as her nipples hardened and strained against her nightclothes' delicate fabric.

Nervous about facing him down.

Nervous about not facing him down.

But Nick made the decision.

"As you wish," he said curtly. He walked to the door, his body silhouetted by the full moon peering through the window.

"You are not a gentleman," Toria snapped.

Nick paused at the door. He looked back at her, appraising her body with his eyes in a way that left no doubt that he desired her, that he could have her if he chose. His hardness swelled against the fabric of his pajama bottoms. His eyes glittered with a predatory glint.

"You're so wrong," he said at last. "Only a very real and very foolish gentleman would leave you like this."

Chapter Eleven

"I trust you have had a restful night after such an exciting wedding day," Special Agent Patricia Rogers said. She unbuttoned her light gray blazer and stared at Toria with unmistakable challenge.

"Well, yes, uh, of course," Toria stumbled over her words, feeling terrible because she was brought up to believe that lying was bad. Always bad. Even lying to someone who was trying to send Nick and Anya back to Byleukrainia.

And she hadn't anticipated this meeting being called so soon after her marriage. The INS sure doesn't fool around, she thought.

"Actually, we didn't get much sleep," Nick said with a lazy, entirely too self-satisfied grin. "You know how it is."

Patricia Rogers pursed her lips in a manner clearly stating that she had no idea how it was and had no intention of finding out.

The two other men in the room, Dean Nash and INS Agent Smith, nodded sagely, not wanting to be titillated by the prospect of questioning the Sankovitch couple on the day after their wedding, Toria presumed. But nonetheless clearly filled with curiosity.

Toria gritted her teeth. "Yes, that's right, we didn't get much sleep," she said, although she had no idea whether Nick slept soundly or restlessly. She had slept very badly.

It had been a long time since sexual feelings of any sort had been aroused within her. Having no romantic relationship, being busy with work, having no desire to seek out titillating material in, say, a risqué movie, she could go days without even thinking about sex. Weeks without more than a passing acknowledgment that, yes, sex existed and some people did it.

Last night, after Nick left her room, she couldn't go two minutes without thinking about it.

Sitting on the bed, however primly, with a copy of some ground-breaking research from the University of Chicago about teaching business English to inner-city kids—all she could think of was Nick stretching out on the sheets like a languorous lion and her sliding on top of him . . .

So much for the University of Chicago research paper.

Next, she had tried organizing her sweater drawer. Her fingers lingered over the cashmere sweater sets handed down from her mother or exotic apparel bought by her father on his trips to research esoteric languages. The tactile excitement tripped off thoughts of the smoothness of Nick's skin, the unyielding quality of his muscles.

She had shoved her drawers back in with a violent jerk.

But against her will she fantasized about what would happen if she just opened up the guest-room door—there were no locks on any of the bedroom doors. Don't say anything, she'd tell him, and then she imagined the wanton satisfaction she'd receive...

Only a little under thirty years of training in being a lady stopped the thought.

It didn't help matters much when Nick climbed into bed with her at six in the morning, wearing a scratchy tweed robe and muttering something about Anya's making breakfast in bed for them.

It could have been an intensely sensual experience, lingering in bed with him. Or it could have been a moment of indignation and propriety—her choice entirely.

But seconds later, Anya had come upstairs with a box of cherry Pop-Tarts and a bottle of orange juice.

So much for her wedding night.

"Well, why don't we get down to business?" Agent Rogers said, pulling out a large file folder and laying it on the conference table in front of her. She looked at Nick. "You have the appropriate documentation?"

"Yes, right here," Nick said, reaching into the pocket of his plaid flannel shirt and producing three copies of the marriage license. He pushed them across the conference table toward Agent Rogers. She looked at them with distaste and shoved them into her folder.

"Mr. Sankovitch," she said exasperatedly. "You managed to get married at exactly—"

"Doctor," Dean Nash interrupted. "Dr. Sankovitch. His Ph.D. is in environmental sciences. He may look like an ordinary workman," he said, wincing only briefly at the mud stains Nick had tracked on the Aubusson carpet. "But he's one of the finest scientists at our small college."

"We know his background," Agent Smith said.

Patricia Rogers looked through her file. "As I was saying, Dr. Sankovitch, you managed to get married at the most opportune time," she said. "If this marriage were to be valid, you and your daughter both would be legally entitled to stay in this country."

"Yes," Nick said cautiously.

"It's such a happy coincidence that the love of your life agrees to be your bride at just the right time," Rogers continued, fingering the copies of the license in her folder. "And to be able to conduct a campus romance without anyone suspecting!"

"We tried to be discreet," Nick said tersely.

"Very discreet," Rogers confirmed. "So discreet nobody knew about it."

"My secretary says she knew they were made for each other," Nash interrupted. "And Nick's—I mean, Dr. Sankovitch's—secretary says she suspected this all along."

Rogers stared at him dismissively. "I don't believe this marriage to be valid," she said, snapping her file folder shut. "What do you think, Smith?"

"Has all the earmarks of fraud," Smith agreed.

Dean Nash cleared his throat. "Now, Agent Rogers, the college has cooperated in many aspects of your investigation during the process of consider-

ing returning Dr. Sankovitch to his country. But I
must point out to you that Dr. Sankovitch and Dr.
Tryon—"

"Sankovitch," Toria corrected. "I'm taking my
husband's name."

Dean Nash did a double take, and Toria realized
that even he had his doubts about this marriage. She
was almost glad he did. Nash had been the dean for
so long, and chairman of the chemistry department
for so many years before that. He was like a family
member. She hated to deceive him. She hoped he
would forgive her once he knew the truth.

But he looked as if he was positively delighted by
the wedding. The warmth he felt for Nick was obvious—he wanted him to stay in the country. He didn't
look unhappy that she was doing her best to help.

"As I was saying, the Sankovitches—both of
them—are the most ethical, intelligent, well-rounded
couple I know," Dean Nash continued. "I'm not
surprised they fell in love. In fact, I think I could have
predicted it. They're made for each other. My wife
has already bought them a wedding present at Mar-
shall Field's. And she's planning on having a small
dinner for them sometime next month—if Toria and
Nick don't have any scheduling conflicts."

Rogers and Smith looked at Nick and Toria in turn.
Toria imagined herself through their eyes and could
well understand their disbelief.

Nick had just returned from another morning in
the muddy waters of the DuPage River. Although he
wore hip boots when he worked, he still had grass
stains on his hands and his shirt. His jeans were worn

and flecked with dirt, his hiking boots traced with mud. He hadn't had time to wash up when he had been summoned to Dean Nash's conference room.

And Toria wore her gauziest antique blouse, with a fragile brooch at its collar. Her hair was pulled back with hairpins into a tight bun and her hands were softened with her familiar rose-scented lotion. She knew she presented herself much like a delicate china figure.

She reached for Nick's dirty hand on the conference table. She hoped the gesture would appear natural and unforced, but Nick looked at her with fatal hesitation and surprise.

He didn't appear to be a man who had—to use impossibly archaic language—taken possession of his wife the previous night.

Out of the corner of her eye, Toria saw Smith smirk at their clumsy hand holding.

"You are to appear at our offices downtown the Monday after next," Rogers announced abruptly. "You'll be interviewed separately as well as together. Please bring whatever supporting documentation you may have—letters, postcards, notes. I hope that you'll prove my hunch wrong. And as for you, Mrs. Sankovitch..."

"Yes?"

"I hope you understand that deceiving the United States government in matters such as this carries a significant penalty, including the possibility of prison time. I suggest you consult an attorney if you have any questions."

Toria's eyes widened at the other woman's crisply delivered warning.

"Congratulations," Smith said. "Uh, I mean, if you really are...you know...in love."

Rogers shook her head.

"Come on, Smith," she ordered, shoving her folder into her briefcase. "Time to go."

"It's all right," Nick murmured as Rogers and Smith were shown out of the room by Dean Nash. "She's just doing her job."

Toria swallowed, her mouth and throat dry. "They're serious, aren't they?"

"Dead serious," Nick confirmed. "They have the Byleukrainian government breathing down their necks and they have Washington to answer to. We are, I might point out, not in love."

"I don't feel so good about this," Toria moaned.

Nick put his arm around her shoulder, crushing the fragile lace edging.

"I've always done the right thing," she said. "I don't want to do the wrong thing."

"And what is the wrong thing?" he asked softly. "Lying to the government? Being sent back to Byleukrainia? Sending Anya back?"

"I don't know which one is worse, but they're all bad."

Nick pulled away from her. His eyes narrowed. His jaw muscles clenched. "I have to do whatever's necessary to protect my daughter," he said ominously. "So, Toria, you must figure out what you're going to do. We have to go all the way."

"All the way?"

"No regrets, no hesitation. You have to be my bride," he said. She looked up at him through glittering tears. "In every way but one, of course. And you have to do it without looking back, without changing your mind." He turned away from her and looked out the floor-to-ceiling windows to the quad. "If you can't do that," he said, "then I will have to leave."

"And take Anya?"

"Of course. That would be the whole point. To protect her from being returned to Byleukrainia. That's always been the point."

Toria roughly wiped tears from her cheeks and followed his gaze out Dean Nash's window. They watched the students pour from the buildings surrounding the quad—the eleven o'clock classes were over. Toria thought of Anya, of what the future would hold for her. What she would be like when she was a young adult—when she was college age.

In the United States.

And then in Byleukrainia.

She remembered the wedding vows she had made yesterday. She realized that those vows meant something to her, something beyond the mere promise to help Nick and Anya. He couldn't know, he shouldn't know, but she was bound to him.

And that bond was greater than that between herself and her country.

And it was a bond not just for the moment. But in sickness and in health, for richer, for poorer, till death... There was nothing in the wedding vows about Agents Smith and Rogers.

She put her hand in Nick's.

"I won't let you down," she said.

THAT NIGHT, the Sankovitches agreed to forget about Rogers and Smith. Or at least try to.

Toria showed Anya and Nick her father's collections of rare paperweights—those that weren't currently on loan to the Art Institute of Chicago. And then Nick insisted on watching reruns of *Gilligan's Island* and *The Brady Bunch*. Toria had been surprised at how much she enjoyed each—she had last seen the shows as a child, at friends' houses. She had forgotten the guilty pleasure.

They had ordered pizza from the local take-out place and Toria had tried one of Nick's beers. Then she sat in bed with Anya while Nick read from a storybook of traditional Byleukrainian fables. And after Anya went to sleep, Toria and Nick worked late into the night exchanging facts, sharing memories and developing a falsified courtship.

The best times, of course, were when she forgot entirely about the cloud hanging over their heads— the upcoming interview with the INS.

Her feelings were sometimes confused as the lines blurred between reality and the life they were creating. Sometimes she even shed a tear, thinking of the rigors of the life Nick had fled. Sometimes she felt nostalgic, thinking of her parents and the "egghead" intellectuals they had entertained so often.

Saying good-night was awkward. Nick kissed her again, chastely on the palm of her hand. As if anything he did could be considered wholly chaste.

But before she could tell him that she thought it was a good idea for him to confine his displays of affection to public occasions, he went into the guest room and closed the door softly.

TORIA SAT UP, shoving aside the linen sheets. She checked the alarm clock—nine o'clock.

What was that terrible racket?

She hastily put on a pair of khaki shorts and a white linen camp shirt, slipping her feet into the white sneakers at the bottom of her closet. In the hall, she noted that Nick's room was empty—his bedsheets were thrown back and a familiar pair of cotton pajama bottoms were abandoned on the floor. She had to stop herself from going in, drawn as she was by the undeniably masculine impression he had made in her feminine lair.

She turned away, though. The line between real and unreal, between intimate couple and partners in deception, was blurred enough. She knew she had to protect her heart and obey her head.

She checked Anya's room and found it empty, as well. Anya had neatly made up her bed and lined up eight Barbies—all in highly fashionable ensembles— on the pillow.

And still, the pounding rhythm of—could it be?— country music.

Toria went downstairs, following the sound through the kitchen and out the back door. She found a boom box on top of the cast-iron table and switched it off.

''Hey!'' Nick yelled.

Toria looked across the lawn and saw Nick on his knees in front of the flower bed. He wore jeans but no shirt, and his muscles glistened as if covered with the dew that clung to the wisps of grass. He stood up and dropped the shovel he had been using.

"Don't you appreciate fine music?" he growled. "That was Billy Ray Vaughan."

"I didn't know you liked country music."

"That's exactly what I like about America. That and hiphop, jazz, rock, blues, even disco. But I've got to listen to country music this morning to get me in the mood."

"In the mood for what?"

"The rodeo."

"Huh?"

Anya appeared from one of the flower beds, her T-shirt and shorts smudged with dirt.

"Naperville's Western Round-Up Days," she said. "After we finish putting in the tulip bulbs, we're going. Aren't we?"

"You've got to be kidding," Toria said. "It's so hokey. We're not a Western town—we're a college town. And we don't have cowboys—never did. It's just a way for the local businesses to make money. Sidewalk sales, a rodeo, everybody wearing cowboy hats. It'll be so crowded, there won't be any parking, and..." Toria searched for more things wrong with the festival.

"Have you ever been to it?" asked Nick.

"No," she admitted.

"You mean you grew up here and you've never gone to the Round-Up Days?" Nick demanded. He winked at Anya conspiratorially. "The first thing we're going to do is buy you a cowboy hat. In the meantime, help us with these bulbs. I found them in the mud room. If we don't plant them soon, they'll rot. You've waited nearly too long."

"I ordered them from a catalog," Toria explained. "I wasn't sure when I'd get the time to plant them."

"This morning sounds just fine," Nick said. "And I assumed you wanted them along the border of these perennials?"

Toria nodded.

Nick held up one of the brown onionlike bulbs. "Tulips are so delicate," he said. "Did you know that the flowers were so prized in the last century that in Holland family fortunes were won and lost over single bulbs?"

"That seems kind of crazy."

"It seems crazy now, but the beauty of the flower is so special, so enchanting, it makes winter disappear—it still is magic, even today, don't you think?"

Toria smiled.

"I guess you're right. They do make the winter go away with their blooms."

"I don't ordinarily plant tulips," he continued. "I am happier with hardier plants, the kind that grow along the riverbank—Queen Anne's lace, black-eyed Susans, and the like. You have them in your garden, back there."

"I've always thought of them as weeds."

"Weeds are only the plants that survive and crowd out others with their exuberance," Nick said. "But there's something to be said for planting a bulb, patiently waiting through the long, cold winter and then protecting a fine shoot for the promise of a single burst of color. They will look good together, your tulips and my weeds.''

They stood together, their hands nearly, but not quite, touching. Hers smooth and white as cream, his callused and bruised and dirty. They looked at the garden, laughed at Anya's chase of an errant butterfly, and it wasn't for several minutes that they realized that they wouldn't share the beautiful garden together.

Spring was a long time away.

And Toria knew that regardless of the outcome of their coming interview, the Sankovitch family wouldn't be here when the first tulips bloomed.

Chapter Twelve

"I'm not wearing a hat," Toria said.

"Come on, you'll look great," Nick begged.

"I'll look like an idiot."

"So?" Anya asked.

"So I have my standards to uphold," Toria replied with mock regalness.

Anya giggled and Nick shook his head.

"You'll look like a beautiful cowgirl," Nick said, handing the vendor a twenty-dollar bill to pay for three hats.

Toria plunked a pink-banded ten-gallon hat on her head and vamped playfully.

"See, what did I say?" Nick demanded, nudging his daughter. "A beautiful cowgirl."

"The most beautiful cowgirl in Naperville," Anya agreed.

"I hope you'll keep in mind, Anya, that there have never been any cowboys or cowgirls in Naperville," Toria warned. "This is just a gimmicky fair."

"You don't like it!" Nick protested.

Toria sighed and shook her head. She found it difficult to admit, but maybe the Round-Up Days weren't as terrible as all that.

"If Anya's having a good time, I suppose it has some redeeming value," she teased.

"I'm having an excellent time!" Anya proclaimed. She put on her hat and ran ahead to a crowd gathering in front of a pantomimist. Nick put on his own hat.

"Think I look like a real American cowboy?" he asked.

Toria looked up at him. If she were honest, she'd tell him that he looked like a pinup. The kind of guy who belonged on a calendar, not on a range.

"You sure don't look like a respected academic," she chided.

"And that's just fine with me. What about you? Can you give up being a 'respected academic' for the day?"

"That's easy. I never think of myself that way to begin with. You do important research and you train graduate students. I just try to get freshmen who aren't ready for college up to speed."

"You still think you're not doing anything important," Nick scolded. "Stop living by your parents' standards. That's what America is all about—making your own standards."

"It's not my parents' standards. You should listen to my colleagues in the department," Toria said lightly. "They think I don't belong in the same department. Of course Missy's really nice about it—she says she likes my classes because when I invite her to do a guest lecture during the semester, she gets to ogle all the hunks from the football team.''

''I think you don't mind the rest of your colleagues' pomposity,'' Nick said, buying some cotton candy and handing her the sticky cone. ''I think it's your parents' approval you're still looking for. You think you have to come out from under their shadow by doing what they did. Come—be like me. Teach others happily and don't worry about how you are regarded by others. Your friends like you, and Dean Nash likes you. Who cares about anyone else?''

''That's easy to say and very hard to do,'' Toria said. ''My father was dean and my mother's work is still quoted in the most important articles in her field. And together, they took this college from a very small school to being one of the best private colleges in the Midwest. I'll never live up to them.''

''I hear how you talk about them, and I know you love them and admire them. But you should remember there are other ways to succeed in life than by living a copy of their lives. You can always fail at being them. You'll only succeed at being you.''

''And who do you think I am?'' Toria challenged.

''A beautiful woman who is very kind, very good to people and who uses her talents to help others,'' Nick said. ''You don't need to apologize for that, and you don't need to change who you are.''

''I don't think of myself as beautiful,'' Toria protested. ''And I don't think of myself as particularly talented. I'm pretty ordinary.''

Nick leaned closer to her, letting his warm breath caress her ear.

"Ordinary. I don't think so, Toria. Maybe you haven't let anyone see you closely enough to appreciate you." He paused as his voice caught. "If you want to get pleasure from a cowboy festival, let yourself. Not every pleasure is subdued, not every good thing is from a book and not everything should be measured by an academic's standard."

"But the college has always been my life. That's part of who I am."

He looked at her thoughtfully. He had such a special gift, Toria realized—the ability to look at a person and focus on him or her totally. He was seeing her and learning about her with an intensity that was absolute.

"Would your parents approve of me?" he asked.

Toria replied cautiously. "They'd approve of doing anything to help another academic maintain his freedom. They worked very hard in the seventies to help academics get out of the Soviet Union."

"But would they approve of me?"

Toria started. He wasn't just talking about their sham marriage. He was asking about himself. As a man. And in a flash, she realized that her parents would see the jeans, the muddy work boots, the impatience with college politics—no, they wouldn't really approve. Though their commitment to tolerance would make them hold their tongues, they had always assumed she would marry a nice bland but brilliant tweedy scholar. Someone with tenure and a pipe. And a couple of articles published in the "right" scholarly journals. Someone who was serious. About his work. About getting married.

''It would depend . . . depend on what your intentions were.''

He put his arm around her waist and drew her to him. The crowd moved, eddying around them like a river.

''My intentions,'' he said, raising her palm to his lips. ''My intentions are always honorable, though sometimes—how did your colleagues put it?—sometimes so primitive. Not quite all-American.''

Her heart thaddumped!

He grabbed her hand and pulled her toward the rodeo tent. Anya caught up with them, laughing as she held her hat to her head.

''Step right up for the adventure of your life!'' A barker, wearing jeans and a Stetson, announced from atop an overturned barrel. ''Limited spaces are available in our lineup of bronco-busting cowboys.''

The barker scanned the crowd, finding no one foolish enough or brave enough to try. Men's eyes skittered away from his brazen stare. Women looked at each other and giggled.

''Come on!'' the barker challenged. ''Where is there a courageous man—or woman—who's willing to match their brains and brawn with a five-hundred-pound baby bronco?''

His words lingered on the crisp air, but he surely didn't expect any of the Midwestern suburbanites to take the challenge. The young married men with their colored polo shirts and the older ones with their plaid shorts, even the teens with T-shirts announcing their rock group allegiances, backed away.

Still, the barker persisted, making it seem as if he was ready to pluck one of them, any one of them, from the crowd. And if the fiendish smirk on his face meant anything, he was relishing his task.

"I'll do it!" Nick yelled suddenly, raising his hand high.

"Nick, don't!" Toria cried.

"No, this'll be just like the old country," he shushed. "We rode yaks all the time."

"But this is a show," Toria explained. "That man isn't seriously asking for cowboys. They use professionals. You'll get yourself killed."

Nick pulled his arm out from under her stern admonition and strode to the front of the crowd. Families pushed aside their baby carriages and teens drew back in order to make way for him. The barker looked down at Nick with frank surprise.

"You're sure, pardner?" he asked. "A man has to be crazy to do this."

"I'm sure I can do it."

"You haven't had a little much to drink, have you?" The barker questioned, leaning forward to whisper discreetly in Nick's ear.

"Oh, no," Nick said loudly. "I'm not drunk and I'm not a lunatic. But I am somebody who loves to try new things."

The barker looked him up and down, appraising his strength and bravery, his foolhardiness and skill, and made his decision.

"Folks!" the barker shouted, arms stretched wide. "Here you have it, a new cowboy, a brave man willing to give it a try, a potential rising star in the rodeo circuit. Anybody else for a try?"

The crowd collectively recoiled.

"Well, then, get your chance to see this cowboy extravaganza right here," the barker continued, pulling out a roll of tickets. "Two dollars for adults, a dollar for kids."

Anya pulled at Toria's arm. "Come on," she said. "Let's go see."

Toria watched as Nick disappeared into the stadium. "Are you sure he knows what he's doing?" she asked.

"My dad? He always knows what he's doing."

"You're just saying that because you're his daughter."

"No, it's true," Anya said. "Cross my heart and hope to die, stick a needle in my pie—he's incredible."

"Eye, Anya, it's eye."

"What do you mean—eye?"

"It's stick a needle in my eye."

"Why would you want to do that?"

They found seats in front, and Toria had to caution Anya several times not to lean over the barriers that separated the audience from the dust-covered field. The P.A. announced the beginning of the rodeo and asked the crowd to welcome the first cowboy. It wasn't Nick, but still, Toria's heartbeat quickened and her mouth went dry. As the cowboy burst from the box on a raging bronco, her terror mounted.

How could Nick possibly do this without getting killed?

She was miserable, utterly miserable, watching cowboy after cowboy ride the bronco—each for less than ten seconds. She wondered how Anya, how the crowd, could stand it. The terror, the suspense, the agony. And yet everyone, including—no, especially—Anya, screamed and cheered and clapped for each contestant.

On an ordinary Saturday afternoon, Toria would have been puttering in her garden, entertaining friends for tea, listening to some nice music or curling up with a good book.

Last Saturday, she had gone into Chicago with a few girlfriends to see the latest exhibit of French Impressionists at the Art Institute. Not that she knew anything about the Impressionists—but at least they were beautiful and it was a relaxing afternoon, followed by a light, early dinner she'd prepared at home. She had been in bed with a murder mystery by ten o'clock.

Oh, how nice and cozy and peaceful her life had been!

Toria pulled her cowboy hat off, its cheap satin ribbon coming undone. She was tired. She was hot. She was frankly worried sick about Nick. And she couldn't see the point of riding an animal that didn't want anyone on its back. Especially when the ride was going to end so quickly and with such a resounding thump as body met ground.

She sat quietly in her seat, unsettled by the pounding of her heart. The shallowness of breath. The slight tremor of her hand as she fiddled with the hat's ribbon.

Why should she care about what happened to Nick? If he landed on his . . .

"And now! Fresh from the ivory tower of North Central College!" the P.A. exclaimed. "Scientist, cowboy, and professor . . . Nicholas Sankovitch!"

One second.

Toria rose from her seat as Nick was ejected from the box, one hand high in the air, one hand firmly on the bronco's bit. Nick's jaw muscles rippled with suppressed power, and his eyes were narrowed to thin slits.

Two seconds.

The bronco flipped up, pirouetted and brutally rammed its body against the plywood walls of the auditorium. A lusty shriek arose from the crowd. Toria's hand went to her collarbone, as if she could quell her fear and excitement with a soothing touch of her fingers.

Three, four, five seconds.

Nick hung on, through brutal kicks and rambunctious jumps. His head jerked back once, and for a bare instant, he seemed to give the crowd an insouciant smile. Hey, this is fun! his twinkling eyes seemed to say. And then the bronco bolted across the stadium. But he could not get out from under Nick's firm grip on his neck. Toria and Anya clung to each other, shrieking their encouragement.

Six, seven, eight seconds.

"Hang on, Nick! Hang on!" Toria called out, waving her hand wildly, though she should have known that Nick couldn't see her. The animal's back hooves kicked up a hurricane of dust and still, Nick clung ruthlessly, his hat long since trampled underfoot. The rodeo clowns cautiously marked a perimeter around the furious bronco.

Nine, ten, eleven seconds.

The bronco jolted right, then left, faked right and then . . . dumped Nick into a cloud of red and brown dust.

"Oh, no," Toria whispered.

The dust rose, the clowns circled nervously around the edges and the crowd held its breath.

Twelve, thirteen, fourteen seconds.

Emerging from the red haze, the bronco galloped in a wild parade around the stadium—with Nick's arms around its neck, his taut legs scissored around the animal's back. A cheer erupted from the bleachers. When they had paraded in a full circle, Nick slid off, a satisfied grin on his face as he hit the dust.

"There you have it, folks!" the announcer crowed. "Eighteen seconds, making the professor Naperville's Round-Up Champion! Let's give him a hand!"

Anya yelled and hopped from foot to foot. Toria clapped madly. The bronco, under the hands of the clowns, trotted away with a self-satisfied smirk on its face.

Nick dusted off his hands and accepted his hat from a passing clown. Other clowns corralled the horse toward the flap leading out of the auditorium. After a brief bow to acknowledge the cheering audience, Nick ran to Toria and Anya.

His face was flushed and sweaty, his skin covered with red dust. But his smile was infectious, and when he leaped up over the stands to Toria, she welcomed his embrace.

Even his kiss.

Their lips met hard, with no preliminaries, no coy hesitation.

This was the kiss of a champion. Accepting his due as a winner from his woman.

He pulled her close to him, and his mouth hungrily sought—and won—his prize.

She responded, surrendering to him as if he were a warrior and she his tender and adoring maiden, sensing the power within him, though probably only the smell of sweat and dirt and danger. The damp of his arm possessing her soaked the fragile cotton of her sundress, the dust at his fingertips soiling the back of her neck.

And then, self-consciousness took her back. Back to her shell of dignified restraint. Her arms, trapped in his embrace, pushed him away. Her head jerked back indignantly. She held Nick's gaze with a challenging one of her own.

"I ride a bronco who throws me off because I am too civilizing an influence," Nick said lazily. "And I kiss a woman who throws me off because I am not civilized enough."

"It's not that," Toria said, good breeding and years of relentless etiquette making her oddly apologetic. "It's just that we're not..."

She meant to say so many things. To tell him that even with the clowns giving a rousing pantomime of

ranch hijinks in the ring, many people still had their
eyes focused on the professorial cowboy—and on her.
And she was embarrassed by such a public display.

She also wanted to tell him that this wasn't appropriate, that they were partners, in a sense, in getting
a green card for himself and his daughter. But they
weren't really married—though inside she was
squelching the niggling voice that insisted that they
were, since they had said the vows and made it so.

Most of all, she wanted to tell him that they weren't
in love.

As she started to put into words everything she
wanted to tell him, her eyes were caught by a man at
the top of the bleachers.

The man who had been at the courthouse.

The man who had been outside her house that
night.

She saw him behind Nick's shoulder—he stood out
because he was wearing a somber gray suit when all
around him were wearing casual gear. And in contrast to the gyrating crowd, he stood quietly, motion-
less. His eyes met Toria's and she shivered.

"Nick," she said.

He started to turn, and instantly she realized that
if he did, the man—an INS agent, no doubt—would
know. Would record their moment in which the deception was revealed.

She touched his cheek and Nick looked at her, his
eyes brilliant and demanding.

Though she didn't consider herself to be tremen-
dously experienced as a woman, on the other hand
she was no childlike virgin. She knew what he would

think of her invitation, but she also knew that if he turned away in curiosity he would blow their cover.

"Kiss me, Nick," she said brazenly.

He didn't need to be asked twice.

Chapter Thirteen

"Toria!" Nick gasped, as he drew back after the most explosive, awe-inspiring, soul-to-soul kiss of his life. His voice dropped to a whisper as he searched for confirmation that she, too, had felt the magic, had been touched by the passion. "Toria, my darling."

Instead of meeting his eyes, she looked at his shoulder—or maybe over his shoulder. He started to turn around, but she insistently held his chin. Anyone near them would have thought it a loving gesture—Nick merely found it baffling.

"Toria, what's going on?"

"Oh...nothing. He's gone."

"What do you mean, he's gone?"

"There was a guy—that guy I've seen before," she said. "Nick, I'm convinced somebody's watching us. Maybe INS is following us."

"I wouldn't be surprised if they were," Nick said, shrugging. Inside, he boiled. So their kiss had only been a sham. She had felt nothing. He felt a wrenching within him—he mustn't let his feelings become confused. She was doing him a favor—just as her parents helped Soviet academics caught behind the Iron Curtain. "So we are being followed?"

"Doesn't that scare you?"

"No, I know that they're trying to deport me. What scares me is them succeeding at returning me to Byleukrainia. Nothing else scares me. Not even broncos," he added with a chuckle.

She didn't seem to like the joke.

"Nick, that man was at the courthouse and I saw him again outside the house—you don't believe me, but it's true—and then, today, he was in the stands, in back, right there, just a few minutes ago."

Nick took her hand from his face and kissed its palm, reminding himself again that he owed her so much, but that love—a man and a woman love—was not to be.

"If he's gone, can I turn around now?"

Toria's eyes held his for a defiant moment, and then, with a flutter of sooty lashes, she looked away. The moment when her eyes could no longer meet his confirmed Nick's hunch and he felt his heart soar. She had felt the magic of the kiss! It might have begun as a ruse, but it had transformed her.

Kisses could do that.

But before he could kiss her again—and again—he had business to handle.

He turned around.

The crowd in the bleachers had thinned somewhat, but there was no man in a gray suit. There were plenty of men wearing richly colored polo shirts and defiantly plaid shorts. And plenty of women in pastel versions of their mates' colored polos, all paired with subdued khakis. Here and there were the occasional T-shirts advertising colleges, rock groups, beers or distaste for politicians. And then there were kids— little ones, big ones, whining ones, laughing ones— none of them looking the slightest bit interested in Nick or Toria.

That was too bad, Nick thought, as he forced the muscles in his hands to relax from fists he hadn't even noticed himself form. Because he had wanted to see, to confront, this hunter.

"He's gone," Toria said at last.

"I'm glad," Nick said.

He turned to her, and—the heat of the kiss receding—found himself really studying her beauty, the way he would an especially enticing flower.

She wasn't the kind of woman that a man would call a knockout at first glance. There wasn't anything flashy about her chestnut tresses, nothing ostentatious about her slim figure. Her smile didn't make a man think of a quick good time with cheap liquor and a few well-chosen compliments.

Toria made a man think marriage and commitment and forever and kisses that were sometimes hot and sometimes steamy and sometimes simply the comfortable opening of one soul to another that can only happen between a man and a wife.

Wait a minute!

She was somebody's wife.

His.

And, in just an instant, as she was distracted by something going on in the pit, he realized he was an idiot.

He was trying to fool the INS and he was the one who was fooling himself.

Because marriages of convenience could never just be convenient marriages. The vows and the promises, even if they were made by a lying tongue, took over their makers and transformed the lies to truths—which was something of a relief to Nick because he never liked deceit in the first place.

But now he had a problem.

A wife.

A wife—now distracted as she waved to someone in the crowd—who thought of their marriage as merely a good deed, a charitable act, a kindness she was extending. And while her womanly core responded to his kiss, Nick could see the layers of prim and proper resistance shielding those feelings so that now she was barely aware of him. Aware of him as a man and not a cause.

He ground his teeth as he thought of her telling friends years from now how she helped a fellow academic escape deportation. Maybe she wouldn't tell anyone—but she would always think of him as a favor, a cause, a good deed.

Nick also knew he was somebody whom she expected would quietly drop out of her carefully ordered life at the proper time. It's what he had promised. But he had made other, more potent promises.

Terrible promises because, even though the judge had been talking a little quickly—moving the ceremony along as fast as he could—Nick had still understood him word for word.

He had promised to love, cherish and honor till death did them part.

A considerably different promise from love, cherish and honor till the green card comes in the mail.

He would have pondered this further, maybe even tried to explain this to Toria—as if she, an American raised on pragmatism, would understand. But out of the corner of his eye, he saw his little mischief-maker Anya in an empty corner of the stadium. A camera crew stood with her, a buxom blond reporter he recognized from the local news show holding a microphone for his daughter who was talking a mile a minute.

"What the...!"

Nick marched across the stadium to Anya.

"What's going on?" he demanded.

"Oh, Professor Sankovitch!" The news reporter cried, shifting her weight from one foot to the other, vainly attempting to stop her high heels from sinking in the dust. "Can we get a short interview?"

"About what?" he demanded.

"Your incredible bronco ride, of course," she replied. "And I also understand that you recently married a local woman?"

He felt Toria near him, her scent now so familiar to him that he didn't need to turn around. But he reached out his hand, and she, seeming to immediately understand him, came into his arms. His other arm he put firmly around Anya's shoulders—more to keep her in line than anything else at the moment.

"Can we just get a few words for the camera?" the reporter asked, adjusting the shoulder pads on her tomato red suit. "Bob, start rolling," she ordered, not even waiting for Nick's consent. "Professor Sankovitch, where did you learn your amazing bronco skills?"

Nick recoiled. One thing he hated about America, maybe the only thing, was the media, the incessant mugging for the camera, the desire for quick celebrity.

"In Byleukrainia, any boy who can't ride would be something of an oddity," he explained curtly.

"But you managed to beat real pros, men who ride the cowboy circuit," the reporter prompted.

"Just having a good day, I guess," Nick said, uncomfortable at comparing himself with others.

"And this is Mrs. Sankovitch?"

"Yes," Toria said.

"When did you marry?"

"Just two days ago," Toria said.

"Wow! That's amazing. How did you meet?"

"They met because of me!" Anya shouted, wiggling out of Nick's hold. "I introduced them. We were going to have to move and—"

"That's enough, Anya," Nick warned. "You'll have to excuse my daughter, she—"

"Toria has this really romantic music box," Anya said. "And whenever I played it, I always thought of Dad and her."

"That's enough, Anya, I'm sure the nice lady would just like to move on," Nick said.

"No, this romance story sounds a lot more interesting," the reporter interrupted. "If you'll pardon me for asking, what happened next?"

"When Dad said we were moving, I thought my dreams would never come true," Anya continued, her words coming out so quickly that she couldn't catch her breath. "But that very night, he told me he had fallen in love with Toria and instead of moving we would be a family."

"Anya!" Nick exclaimed. He tugged his daughter by the shoulder and hustled her toward the stadium exit. "Thank you for the interview," he said over his shoulder.

"Well, I wonder what his problem is?" the reporter harrumphed.

"You'll have to excuse Nick," Toria said, although she had no idea how or why anyone should. She raced to catch up with them outside the rodeo. "What was that all about?" she asked.

"Anya shouldn't have said anything," Nick said gruffly.

"You didn't have to be rude," Toria pointed out.

"You don't understand," Nick said.

"Why were you so upset? You were so happy about winning, I thought surely you'd—"

Nick abruptly turned around, pulling Toria close to him. She felt his hot breath against her cheek.

"Her story is quite different from the one we told at the wedding reception," he whispered. "How are you going to explain that?"

"I don't know."

"Well, let's hope that interview never airs."

"I don't think it will after how impolite you were."

He relinquished her, and as a measure of how strongly he had held her, she lost her balance momentarily. He reached out to steady her, she recoiled and their eyes locked.

"I don't think I'll have to explain anything to the INS," Toria said. "I think they'll ask us a few questions and they'll leave Anya out of it."

"How little you know," Nick sighed.

Anya pulled at his arm, and his dark emotions instantly disappeared.

"Daddy, I'm sorry," she said. "I always talk too much, don't I?"

"No, sweetie, you talk just the right amount," Nick said, patting her hand. "But maybe you could quiet down just a little?"

"I promise," Anya said, flicking her hands across her chest in the time-honored cross-my-heart-hope-to-die way.

"Now, why don't you go pick up my prize?" Nick said. He nodded in the direction of the barker announcing the next hour's show.

Anya shot off, pigtails flying behind her, a ribbon coming loose and falling to the ground.

Nick shook his head as he watched her. "Patty Cook, Lark MacPhail, Mary Walsh and Julia Grace," he said sadly.

"Huh?"

"The names of your three best girlfriends in kindergarten," he said. "Patty moved away to Little Rock, Lark married a lawyer from New York, Mary is a housewife in Cleveland and Julia works as a bartender in San Diego. You exchange Christmas cards and see each other about once a year."

Toria smiled. "You're really good."

"Yeah, but am I good enough?" Nick asked darkly. "Remember, in order to do this, we're lying to everyone we know. Our colleagues, our friends, my daughter. And it won't make a bit of difference if we get tripped up by something like what happened in there."

"I don't like lying," she said.

"In any other kind of world we wouldn't have to," he said, smiling ruefully. "We're the only two people in the world who can know that we don't love each other madly."

She flinched but recovered quickly. "We're the only ones who can know we aren't passionate about each other," she said archly, swallowing the lump in her throat.

He slipped his hand in hers, the dust and sweat from his fingers mixing with the trace of lotion she used.

"When we hold hands, only we know we don't mean it," he said, torturing himself with the words.

He looked for signs that she might disagree with his words, that she might think of the marriage vows as having a life of their own.

He leaned forward to kiss her. He watched her eyes, waiting for the moment of surrender when a woman closes her eyes to the intense feelings.

But she kept her gaze steadily on his.

Their lips pressed dryly. And Nick tore himself from her before his torture was complete, before he hurt himself with feelings that again went beyond gratitude.

"And when we kiss, we do it only for show," she said coolly as he pulled away. "And no one knows we don't feel anything."

He gulped.

He'd misread her. Had he only wished so hard to see love in her eyes that he had fooled himself? How ironic if his marriage fooled no one, except for him.

Thank heaven for Anya, he thought, as she nearly knocked them over.

"Dad! Toria! Look at it! It's the biggest, most beautiful trophy in the whole world!"

THAT AFTERNOON, they came home exhausted—loaded down with teddy bears won at the basketball booths, half-eaten bags of popcorn, and the nickel-plated trophy cup with a cowboy hat engraved on its side. The mailman had left three wedding presents: a crystal bowl from Missy, a set of eight pearl-handled dessert forks from Dean Nash and his wife, and a toaster from Nick's secretary. Toria put them in the hall closet along with all the other wedding presents. Someday she'd have to figure out whether to write thank-you notes or return them or both.

Anya flopped down on the couch in front of the TV and yawned loudly.

Toria went upstairs to take a quick shower before dinner. As she threw her clothes in the laundry basket, she stretched her tired muscles. It had been a long day, but one that—the tension between her and Nick aside—had been wonderful.

Who would have thought she could have so much fun doing something so new!

She glanced up at the mirror. She was a slender woman, but with generous curves that weren't always what the latest fashion demanded. Her breasts were high, nipples tilted gently upward, her stomach flat and her buttocks rounded.

She seldom thought much about her body—never having had the discipline for daily workouts or the patience for prolonged self-admiration. But whenever she was confronted by herself, whether in the bathroom mirror or the dressing room of a store, she was reasonably happy with what she saw. Maybe not model quality, but she was content.

But now she noticed something that hadn't been there before or hadn't been noticeable. There was an untried quality to her body—as if she were a racehorse that had never run the track, as if she were a butterfly not yet fully out of her cocoon.

She wanted a husband, wanted a baby—wanted her breasts to have the fuller, rounder quality of motherhood, even anticipated when her stomach would lose its boyish flatness.

She wanted someone whose touch was familiar to her, whose kiss at the back of her neck was both exciting and comforting, who could bring her to heat in moments or take his sweet tormenting time.

To all outward appearances, she had it all. A husband downstairs—she could hear him puttering around the kitchen. A daughter—watching television in the living room. But they were both only on loan.

And of course, she thought as she slipped into a pale yellow sundress, this family was counterfeit. A deceit. A lie.

She walked downstairs and flipped off the television as she noticed that Anya was asleep. She had nothing, really, she reminded herself as she gently slipped Anya's sneakers from her feet and pulled a quilted throw over her bare legs.

She looked back at the television, realizing that the set now looked as if it had always been there, as if it belonged. She smiled wistfully at the trophy cup that Nick no doubt had put on top of it, a bouquet of Queen Anne's lace and tender blue hydrangeas arranged haphazardly in it.

Chapter Fourteen

Leaving Anya on the couch to sleep off the exhaustion of the Round-Up Days gave the adults plenty of time for a quiet dinner on the screened porch at the back. Toria flung a piece of Battenburg lace over the braided twig table and put out an elegant but simple mélange of fruit, cheese and hearty bread. She didn't mean the food to be so enticing—it was just what was in the fridge. Nick uncorked a bottle of red wine and sat down, the delicate wicker chair groaning under his muscular frame.

"I've never felt more at home," he said.

The words seemed so poignant to Toria as she laid out the delicate rose-patterned plates and the mother-of-pearl-handled forks and knives.

This isn't your home, she thought, *and it's not going to feel like my home any longer when you leave.*

But instead of focusing on what she had to lose in the coming months, she promised herself to live in the present.

She lit a few candles and put them on the table. They were purely functional—she hadn't gotten the back porch light fixed. But the effect—of lace and delicate china, of candles and delicious food—was pure romance.

She didn't mean to make it happen! she thought as he held out her chair for her.

All the pleasures of new marriage haunted the two as they ate and shared a few glasses of the wine.

What was intended to be a working dinner—exchanging facts and quizzing each other—quickly became... too much fun and much too close.

He told her about the one-room schoolhouse he had been educated in—and the teacher who had quickly figured out that Nick had potential. He'd been sent away to the capital, to a state-run prep school, when he was eight. His interest in the environment had come when he had been given the chore of helping clear away the dirt and debris in the sprawling campus. Preserving the tender shoots of wildflowers and the regal spruces became his mission. Nick told her about the next stage of his education, when he helped the farmers to grow their crops.

She told him more about her parents' devotion to the college, about parties for visiting academics, about looking after her parents even before their declining years. Her father often became so engrossed in research that he had to be reminded to eat, and her mother had been so busy with campus-related affairs that Toria had sewn her own school-play costumes by the time she was eight.

"We've grown up worlds apart," Nick said. "And yet, our lives had so many parallels."

"How so?"

"Responsibilities taken on—maybe too young. A desire to help others. A hunger for all the world has to offer, and maybe, just maybe, a little loneliness."

"But there are differences," Toria pointed out. "We're opposites, remember? You're a risk taker and I'm not."

"That's not so bad. You create a wonderful home, a sanctuary, really."

The candles flickered and died. The wine bottle was finished. The food had been eaten.

When Anya woke up and joined them, Toria made her a grilled-cheese sandwich. Nick fixed her chocolate milk.

Then Toria said she was going to bed early. Nick said he would join her later. Toria took that to mean that he would do as they had been doing—he would wait until Anya went to sleep and then he would go to the guest room.

He kissed Toria on the cheek. Anya didn't seem to notice, although Toria knew the kiss was for her benefit.

Toria was relieved as she slipped into her nightgown and readied for bed. It was difficult to be so intimate with a man—*my God,* she thought, *he knows me better than any ever has*—when their arrangement was purely business.

At least it had to be for Nick.

Settling into a warm bed with a mystery, Toria barely heard the tap-tap-tap at her door.

"Toria," called the urgent whisper.

She reluctantly took her eyes from the page in front of her. "Who is it?"

"It's me—Nick. Can I come in?"

"Sure," she answered cautiously, putting her bookmark in place. She looked at him guiltily—she had promised, absolutely promised, that tonight she'd work on her love letters to him. But everything she wrote sounded stilted and unnatural—much like the first few term papers of her remedial English students.

He still wore the clean, faded-to-white jeans he had changed into before dinner and a forest green linen shirt. *I could get myself into real trouble,* Toria thought as her eyes lingered on his features. *He's just too darned sexy for his own—my own—good. How could I be reading a nice little English murder mystery when I could just stare at him?*

She wondered if now would be a good time to take out her paper and pen—but she'd die rather than have him actually watch her write love notes about his sexual charms.

Apparently unaware of her hormone-driven thoughts, he leaned back against the closed bedroom door, hands splayed casually on his hips.

"Anya won't go to sleep," he announced.

Well, I'm not going to get any sleep, either, Toria thought. "That isn't any wonder," she said coolly instead. "We let her nap until seven." Toria touched the buttons on the top of her nightgown, reflexively checking to see if every one of them was done up.

"Why don't you go for another drive?" Toria asked. "It seemed to work the last time just fine."

"I can't. I had wine with dinner. And even if I hadn't, I'm just too tired out. That might have been only thirteen seconds on a bronco, but it's starting to feel like hours.''

"So what's she doing?"

"I told her she can't watch TV this late. But I said she could read.''

"Where's she reading?"

"In her bedroom. I thought perhaps she might drift off to sleep in an hour or so.''

"An hour? And what are you going to do?''

"I hoped I could lie down and read this book,'' he said, holding up a volume she recognized as her father's study on the differences between ancient Greek dialects. ''I thought I should get to know your family's literature. This book is considered the most important one in the field.''

"Yes, I know,'' Toria said dryly. ''It's also not very easy reading.'' She looked doubtfully at the space on the bed beside her.

"I get the impression you don't want me to lie down,'' Nick said, and he looked around for somewhere else to read. In Toria's room, that would only mean one thing—the vanity stool, large enough for Toria's petite frame but almost like a doll's chair to him.

"What about the sofa downstairs?'' Toria asked uneasily.

"It's eleven o'clock at night,'' Nick pointed out. ''She thinks we're in love, that we're a couple. We're supposed to be together. Remember?''

Toria scrunched up on one side of the bed. ''All right,'' she conceded. ''But you stay on your side of the bed, don't get under the covers and do not—repeat, do not—fall asleep." She said all this with more sternness than she ever intended. But she felt oddly determined to keep the delicate distance between them, especially after an evening when they had been so close that she had many times forgotten that they were getting to know each other purely for one purpose.

They couldn't sleep in the same bed, mustn't sleep together!

The intimacy of words, of shared histories, of knowing about each other's routines, and likes and dislikes was in itself becoming acutely difficult. How much more so when contrasted with the loneliness that was going to follow. She was actually going to miss Nick's fast food and fondness for reruns, his booming voice, his enthusiasm and wit. She didn't want to add missing his lovemaking to her list. Because making love would be a disaster.

For him, it might only be a conquest, a memory, an interlude. For her, it would be a stripping away of the thin layer of singleness that remained between them. She would be married to him—in law, in body, in spirit. And nothing, not even their intended "amicable" divorce, would change that. For her.

Fool, she thought with sudden harshness.

"Come on, it's all right," she said, making room for him.

If she sounded too hard-hearted about where he might rest, Nick was either too tired or too grateful to notice. He slipped off his shoes and lay down on the bed with a contented sigh. Trouble was, he took up three-quarters of the bed without meaning to!

He opened her father's book and stared at the title page for several minutes. Toria tried to concentrate on her paperback—but the question of whether the butler or the duchess had shot the duke was simply not interesting anymore.

"Is the television on?" she asked.

Nick groaned.

"Yeah," he said. "I forgot to turn it off. I can't get out of bed too easily. That bronco riding was a little rough on me. My back hurts so bad."

"I'll go turn it off."

He rubbed his shoulders and leaned his head back.

"When you come back upstairs, you wouldn't be interested in massaging my, uh . . ."

"I think not," Toria said curtly.

"You're right. It was presumptuous of me to ask," Nick said. He turned over on his side. His strong back hid his reading. "You're absolutely right, you know. It would be a mistake. I'm sorry."

"Make sure you don't go to sleep," Toria reminded him.

"I won't. This book is too fascinating and I'm in too much pain. I couldn't get to sleep if I tried, even though I think I've been up for nearly twenty hours. I started at four this morning to get your ground mulched for the bulbs."

"I'm grateful—it would have taken me days."

"Grateful enough for a short back rub?"

"Dream on."

"Never hurts to be persistent."

Toria couldn't help smiling. They were bantering like an old married couple!

The all-American scent of Ivory soap clinging to him after his shower. The comfortable way the mattress shifted to accommodate him, as if her furniture had known the man in her life before she did. The way the house seemed full, just full enough—not cavernously empty as it had just a few short days ago.

Live in the moment, her inner voice cautioned, just as thoughts of how she'd miss her make-believe family intruded.

She opened the door, careful to not let it squeak in case Anya was dozing. Downstairs, the weatherman was just finishing up his report of warmer temperatures and was ad-libbing with the anchor. Toria smiled as she recognized the tomato red suit and the frosted blond hair. She had been just this close to a real celebrity!

"That was a wonderful story about Naperville's Round-Up Days," the weatherman said.

Toria nearly called out to Nick and Anya to say that they had just missed the news. It didn't sound as if Anya and Nick were featured. The anchor began reporting some new scandal in Washington, so Toria flipped off the switch. Then she tiptoed upstairs.

Anya looked up from her reading as Toria passed her door. "Aren't you tired, sweetheart?" she asked.

"Not yet," Anya said. "Just let me get to the end of this chapter. It's a really cool book, about seven girls who form a club to make money baby-sitting."

"I think I've heard about those books," Toria said. "And they sound really interesting. But you've got to get some sleep, Anya."

"All right, I promise. Oh, and Toria?"

"Yes, honey?"

"Is it okay if I don't always call you Mom?"

Toria hoped that the beating of her heart, which seemed so explosive to her now, couldn't be heard. "Sure, that's okay," she said cautiously.

"I know I said I wanted to call you Mom when you and my dad got married. But it's kind of scary. I still want to think of my mom, even if I don't remember her. I know you'll be my mom for many more years than she ever was, but I still want to think that she might be watching over me in heaven. Is that bad?"

"Oh, honey, no!" Toria cried. "I'll never take her place. And, you're right, she's probably watching you from heaven." She rushed to Anya's side, and the little girl put her arms around Toria's neck and held on tight.

"You will take the place of a mother, though," Anya said. "I'm going to be spending a lot more time with you. You will be the one who will teach me everything about becoming a woman."

Oh, no, Toria thought wistfully, and she wondered if she and Nick were doing the right thing.

"I was always so scared of the fighting," Anya continued.

"The fighting?" Toria asked, wondering if there had been some domestic problems that Nick had hidden from her.

"You know, the bombs especially, but also when the troops of one side or another would come through town," Anya continued. "One day, in our nursery school, some soldiers were coming through and our teacher hid us in the bathroom and we had to be absolutely quiet for three hours while the soldiers searched the school. They didn't find us. We were very good at being quiet."

Toria didn't even want to ask what the soldiers had been looking for, or what kind of bravery it would have taken for nursery-school children to have the discipline to stay quiet to elude those soldiers.

"It's not like that here," Anya concluded.

"You're right, it's not. It won't ever be that way for you again," Toria said, and she smoothed away the wild locks of hair that had fallen to Anya's forehead.

Just like Nick's, she thought fondly, with a rebellious cowlick.

She held on to Anya, wishing she could take away every hurtful or scary experience the young girl had ever known.

"Can I finish my chapter now?" Anya asked.

Toria laughed and relinquished her little friend. "Sure, just remember to turn off the lights when you're done."

Toria returned to her own room and decided she'd go back to the safe little mystery novel she'd been reading. The butler. The duchess. The creepy wine cellar.

"She'll probably be asleep in ten minutes," she said to Nick, as she softly closed the bedroom door behind her. "By the way, she must have gotten on TV tonight... Nick? Nick?"

He was sound asleep, his face made boyish in sleep, so much younger without the cares of the world—and he had never gotten past the title page of her father's most respected book.

"I should be mad at you," she whispered, as she closed the book and put it on the vanity. "I should wake you up right now and tell you that you have to sit on that little stool over there until she falls asleep."

Instead, she went to her side of the bed, slid under the covers, opened her mystery and tried to interest herself in the butler's alibi.

As soon as Anya went to sleep, she promised herself, she'd slip into the guest room and go to sleep herself.

It had been such a long day.

Chapter Fifteen

Toria bit into a grape-leaf-covered ball of rice and closed her eyes, loving every sensual moment of her dining experience. The lilting flute music, punctuated with insistent cymbals and drums. The scent of cardamom, cinnamon and faint perfumes. The texture of every surface—napkins, wall hangings, the very cushion upon which she sat—rich and brocaded with deep, vibrant color.

Toria felt as if she had been swept up into an exotic fairy-tale land, although Nick had merely driven them into Chicago to a small storefront Byleukrainian restaurant.

Toria loved it, appreciated the adventure. Funny how being with Nick was opening up that side of her personality.

Anya wasn't quite as pleased.

"Do I have to eat this?" Anya whispered, leaning over the table laden with bowls of pickled beets, crushed chick peas and eggplant and shredded meat. "It's gross."

"It's traditional Byleukrainian food," Nick said patiently, heaping a piece of bread with meat and cheese. "You should learn to at least tolerate it."

"Why? I'm an American now," Anya said.

"You're an American first, but you'll always have Byleukrainia in your heart," Nick corrected.

"Do you have Byleukrainia in your heart?" Anya demanded.

He nodded. "I will never forget the country we were born in," he said. "Someday when times are better, we may even go back to see it. And while America has many good things about it, I won't forget everything about Byleukrainia. I'd like to keep what is good about the two countries."

"Yeah, well, this isn't too good," Anya quipped, pointing to a bowl of jellied herring.

"Maybe not," Toria said. "But you might like the bread and the cheese. Why don't you try some of that?" She reached for the small serving plate to give to Anya, and her hands met his. There was a sharp current of electricity in the touch. She looked at him. And then looked away.

She could still feel his touch.

It was the same touch as that morning. . . .

Although two weeks had passed, it wasn't any easier to get up from the same bed this very morning than it had been the first. Luckily, Anya always appeared with breakfast—she had graduated from bringing them Pop-Tarts and juice to enticing them with finer delicacies.

This morning she brought a banana, two cans of Diet Coke and a bowl of Lucky Charms.

As on so many mornings, Toria had said nothing when she awoke with Nick's arm flung over her hips, and he had said nothing about her slender leg curled around his muscular thigh.

Without much more than a brusque good-morning under Anya's watchful gaze, he had grabbed a soda can and retreated to the guest room to dress.

Looking exasperatedly into her mirror while munching the banana, Toria had quickly tugged her most conservative dress from her closet.

Her choice had been the right one, because now, even with her arms covered, her hem at the bottom of her calves and her neckline nearly up to her chin, Toria felt the covert glances, the openmouthed stares from the other patrons of the restaurant.

Only men sat at most tables. At the tables that included women, those women wore long, shapeless robes and scarves that covered their hair. Some even had a black veil to hide all but their kohl-lined eyes. Far from being made somber by their dark, modest clothes, these women laughed and chattered delightedly in the Byleukrainian dialect. But their eyes never directly met those of the men they were with.

Toria wasn't the sort of woman to stand up on her chair to shout and condemn the oppression of women, but she did feel quite uncomfortable.

As their meal progressed, she sensed she was getting even more attention from the whispers carried over the lilting, repetitive music and the indiscreet pointing from behind the tiny Turkish coffee cups. Several mirrors shaped in the traditional Arabic arches accentuated the feeling of being scrutinized from every direction.

"You're not having a good time," Nick observed.

"I'm being stared at," she said. "And I'm not just being paranoid."

"I know. I'm sorry for that. This is the only restaurant in the city that serves our food," he said. "I wanted you to know more about my culture."

"How did you even know this place was here?" Toria asked. There had been no sign in front of the boarded-up storefront.

"There are not many Byleukrainians in Chicago, so everybody knows everything."

"Can we go to Burger King when we're done?" Anya whined.

While Toria shushed her, a man at the next table stood up, his chair bumping against Nick's shoulder. Nick looked up and said something noncommittal in his language. Toria waited for the apology—but the man bumped his chair into Nick's shoulder again, clearly on purpose. Several men gave up all pretense of disinterest and stared openly.

"Anya, come sit on my lap," Toria said nervously.

Anya, looking at her father and the man towering over him, quickly obeyed. She buried her head in Toria's shoulder. Toria could feel the little girl shivering like a captured bird. The music stopped abruptly, leaving behind only the clatter of dishes being washed in the back room.

Nick stood up, at his full height a clear three inches above the man who had bumped him.

The man quietly said something to Nick, and yet everyone in the restaurant could hear him and understood exactly what he meant.

Everyone except Toria.

The man repeated himself.

And Nick punched him—dropping him to the ground like a popped balloon.

"Toria! Go!" he commanded, just as chaos broke out.

Men leaped from their seats toward Nick. Women shrieked and tables were overturned. Plates and glasses shattered on the floor amid angry shouts and hostile cries.

Toria pushed Anya from her lap and grabbed her wrist. She dragged the girl through the melee. The door, covered with posters of action movies with Byleukrainian text, wouldn't give, even when Toria rammed it with her shoulder. Searing pain coursed down her arm. She gritted her teeth and tried again.

Twice, three times, the door just wouldn't open. She looked back at the men surrounding what had been their peaceful table.

She took a deep breath and turned to try again at the door and found herself face-to-face with one of the women from the table beside theirs. A veil covered her face, but Toria thought—no, prayed—that she saw something friendly in the eyes.

The woman pulled a key out of the voluminous folds of her robe. She unlocked the door, shoved Toria and Anya through it and slammed it shut again.

"Thank—" Toria cried out.

But there was no reply.

She blinked to adjust to the sunny urban landscape. She heard the click of the door locking behind them.

"What do we do now?" Anya asked.

Toria looked down at her tear-streaked face, felt the shivering of Anya's shoulders through her cardigan.

Her first job was to get Anya to safety.

Her second job was to help Nick—although from what little she had seen, he deserved everything he got.

After all, he had essentially started it by throwing the first punch. Muttering to herself what an idiot he was, she led Anya the half block down the street to the pickup. After Anya slid into the seat, Toria turned back, wondering what she should do now.

Should she go back in? Should she call the police? Should she do nothing? Although doing nothing was not her usual response to trouble.

The question was answered for her as the restaurant's door opened and Nick strode out. He might have been any other man leaving a restaurant after a fulfilling meal—except his shirt was torn, he sported a wicked cut over his right eye and he had forgotten the navy jacket that he had worn just for the occasion.

As he approached the truck, he handed her the keys.

"I can't see very well and the swelling's only going to make it worse," he said. "But we should get out of here as soon as possible."

"That was pretty stupid of you," Toria said.

"Just drive us home," he said curtly. He got in the passenger side, next to Anya, and pulled a first-aid kit out of his glove compartment.

Toria got in the driver's side and started the truck.

"What did they say that got you so upset?" she asked.

"Just drive," Nick ordered, dabbing his forehead with the gauze bandage.

Toria slowly pulled out of the parallel park. Suddenly, the storefront door blasted open and a half dozen angry men who had fought with Nick came out. Shouting. Waving their arms with upraised fists, brave declarations and fierce indignation.

"I said drive!" Nick shouted.

Toria slammed her foot on the accelerator and the truck jerked past the angry knot of men. One reached out to smash his fist against the taillight—cheers followed.

After three blocks, Toria checked the rearview and realized there was no one following them—still, she felt shaken. She loosened her fingers on the steering wheel—her knuckles were white. Anya's grip on her arm was so tight that Toria's right hand was falling asleep.

Nick staunched the blood on his cut and put the first-aid kit back in the glove compartment. He gave her grunts meant as instructions on how to reach the highway. Toria didn't feel safe until they were on the Eisenhower Expressway, well on their way back to Naperville.

Anya at last relinquished her hold on Toria's arm.

"What did they say that made you so angry?" Toria asked again.

Nick shook his head. "Nothing for you to worry about," he said.

"Anya, do you know?" Toria asked.

Anya shook her head. "We try always to speak English at home, for practice, so I couldn't understand everything they said," she gulped. "Besides, they were talking so fast."

Toria glanced over Anya's head to Nick. "That was pretty stupid," she said again. "You acted like an animal. I mean, so the guy bumped his chair into yours. Couldn't you have resolved with words whatever problem you had with those guys?"

"It wasn't that kind of a problem," Nick said quietly.

He kept his eyes, dark and brooding, on the road.

"Well, what kind of problem could you have that you'd have to punch somebody? He bumped his chair into you. If he didn't say excuse me, why didn't you just say it? Polite people do that."

Nick shrugged and deliberately turned his head away from hers.

"This isn't going to work," Toria said softly. "I can't go out in public with you if you're going to act like that."

"It wasn't what you think."

"Then what was it?"

"I can't tell you," Nick said. "Maybe later, if you're absolutely determined to hear it."

"Oh, so it's me," Anya said petulantly. "How come I don't get to hear it?"

"It's not the sort of thing a girl should know about," Nick said in such a dark voice that even Anya knew not to say another word.

They did not speak again until they pulled into the driveway of Toria's little farmhouse. Nick got out of the truck and gave Anya two dollars, telling her to take her bike down to the drugstore three blocks away and buy him a pack of gum.

"I never get to hear the good parts," Anya protested.

"You should have just enough change to buy yourself an ice-cream bar," Nick said, without responding to her charge.

Anya's face brightened. "Oh, boy! Real food!" she exclaimed, taking the money. She grabbed her bike and pedaled down the driveway.

Nick watched her go and then abruptly went into the house. Toria followed him. He pulled off his torn shirt and threw it into the kitchen garbage can. His back glistened with sweat. He turned around, challenging her with his eyes.

"So—you're determined to know what started the fight?"

"Yes, I think I have a right to know what turned you from a fairly decent gentleman into an animal."

He flinched and turned away, picking up a bar of soap by the sink and making a show of lathering up his face and arms. Toria took a tea towel from a drawer. He rinsed, mumbled something and grabbed the towel from her.

"What?" Toria demanded.

Nick looked up from the towel—with the blood washed away and his hair slicked back from the water, the jagged cut looked angry and painful. She reached out to the swollen skin at its edge. He jerked back but stilled to her soothing touch.

"I'll get bandages," Toria said softly, and pulled out the first-aid kit from below the sink. "Sit down."

He sat at the kitchen table, and she used three bandages to cover his cut.

"Are you hurt anywhere else?"

"No."

But Toria could see angry swelling on his right forearm. He still had a bruise on his shoulder from the previous day's bronco ride. She touched the bruise and looked away.

"You're so physical," she said. "I mean, that bronco riding yesterday. The fight today. What am I supposed to think of you? I'm the kind of person who likes quiet and peace and thoughtfulness."

He took a deep breath. "They made a comment about...you," Nick said. "And me. Their anger was directed at me."

Toria stared at him openmouthed.

"What did they say?"

"They said I was either a traitor or a fool to be with you."

"A traitor because I'm not a Byleukrainian?"

Nick nodded. "And that's not a charge to be taken lightly," he said. "They meant it."

"So what can they do about it now that we're already married?"

He shrugged. "I don't know."

"They also said you were a fool. How come?"

He grimaced—at first she thought because of the pain as he shifted in his chair. Then she realized it had nothing to do with physical pain.

Physical pain Nick could handle. Other things were harder.

"A fool because American women are supposed to be..." He looked away.

"What? Supposed to be what?" She was pushing him, she knew it. But the fight had been deeply disturbing, making Nick seem to be almost a savage. Primitive, that's the word Missy had used.

"Nick, tell me," she said.

He raised his hands to the sky in exasperation. "American women are supposed to be loose, all right? You're the one who wanted to know. And I'm supposed to be a fool because you might be with other men. Are you satisfied that you know what they said?"

Toria shuddered. "Is that everything they said?"

"There's more, but that's enough for you to get the general idea."

Toria stood up and paced around the kitchen. "What a terrible thing! Those men are awful. Is that what everybody in that restaurant was thinking about me? About us?"

"Yes," Nick admitted. "Byleukrainian culture is very old-fashioned."

"Repressive," Toria corrected.

"Old-fashioned," Nick repeated. "They believe in no sex until their wedding, parents arrange marriages, they have no tolerance for adultery and they believe in marrying only within the Byleukrainian community.''

''They believe in being jerks!''

Nick shrugged. ''Some of the extremists, yes, they're very bad.''

''And they're thinking that all American women are...''

''Modern,'' he supplied. ''That's a better word for it.''

''I'll bet that isn't a direct translation of the word they used.''

''Okay, it isn't quite the word they used,'' he conceded. ''*Loose* is closer to what they meant. But American women are modern, and you would call yourself a modern American woman, wouldn't you?''

''Just what is that supposed to mean?''

Nick opened his mouth to explain, and then, seeing that he was on dangerous ground, closed it again.

''Does that mean you agree with them?'' Toria accused.

''Of course not,'' he said quickly.

They stared at each other for several long, searing minutes.

''I thought you said that you made love to Anya's mother without the benefit of marriage,'' Toria said tartly. ''You don't live up to your own old-fashioned ideas.''

''That was different. That was wartime. We were kids who knew our lives could be cut short. We were grabbing the moment because we knew we didn't have the benefit of a stable, secure life.''

"And, of course, I can never understand that. Because I'm an American.'' It was said as an accusation, although she hadn't meant it to sound so harsh. But there it was, between them.

"You don't know me at all,'' Toria said quietly. "You may know who I ate lunch with in second grade and where I went to camp in eighth, but you don't know anything about me. What's inside me. And I don't know much about you. You were absolutely right. We come from different cultures, different worlds. We're complete opposites.''

Nick looked at the floor. She waited, wishing he would say something to deny the truth. But he didn't.

"I'm going to the office,'' she said. "I have tomorrow's class to get ready for.''

She went to the living room to pick up her briefcase and purse. As she slammed the front door behind her, she thought she might have heard him say "You're right.'' But she didn't turn around to ask him if he had.

AT THE OFFICE, she found it difficult to concentrate. She made a pot of tea. She snipped the dying ends from the fern that hung in the corner of her office. She read through several memos from the chairman of the department. When she finished them, she made each one into a paper airplane and glided them into the wastebasket. She organized her bookshelves and sat on the faded rose-upholstered armchair by the window.

All the while she talked to herself.

She agreed that her life was in chaos. She usually prepared lessons weeks in advance, and now she was just managing to keep a day ahead. She usually read several novels during the week—and she hadn't picked up a book in days. She never, ever watched Schwarzenegger films or reruns of sixties sitcoms, didn't drink McDonald's shakes, didn't eat burgers and especially never went to rodeos. All of which she had been doing recently. Basically, she concluded, her life was a shambles.

"Missy calls him definite hunk material," she said. "But he's the exact opposite of everything I've ever wanted in a man. She should be the one with him."

You don't want that, an inner voice calmly replied.

"He's a jerk with ideas right out of the Neanderthal era," Toria said, surprised at how petulant she sounded. "A primitive," she added for good measure.

No, he is desperately trying to understand American ideas of freedom and equality, that annoyingly reasonable voice responded.

"Well, this marriage isn't going to last much longer anyhow," she said. "He gets his green card, we get a divorce and, while I'll miss Anya, she'll still be around. And I'll have my house back. I'll have my life back."

Do you really want that life back?

She reached out to the music box, winding it up and putting it back on the table. The soothing, tinkling waltz distracted her. She let her eyes linger on the dancers.

The cavalry officer glided his beloved around and around the music-box dance floor. He never stepped on his partner's toes. His hands never strayed in an ungentlemanly way. His smile never wavered, his adoring eyes never leaving his partner's face.

Toria looked more closely, noting the rakishness in his eyes but also seeing a longing, bittersweet and tender.

She abruptly stood up.

"I'm never going to get these exams graded!" she declared. "And it's all that man's fault! I'll be so glad when he leaves!"

She took out a piece of stationery and a fountain pen from the middle drawer of her desk. "I'd better get this over with," she said with a grimace. She held her pen poised for an instant as she considered how to start.

Dear Nick,
I don't love you at all. Not one tiny bit. You're crude and unmannerly and I'll be glad when you're gone.

As soon as she finished, she crumpled up the paper and threw it against the wall. She pulled out another piece of stationery.

Dear Nick,

This is supposed to be a love letter, but I can't possibly write a love letter to someone like you.

This would take a while.

"GOOD EVENING, Nicholas Sankovitch," the voice said in Byleukrainian. "We've been watching you for a very long time. We saw you on television yesterday evening. And we tried to talk sense to you this afternoon at the café."

Nick gripped the phone, resisting the urge to yank the cord out of the wall, hoping to avoid what he knew was coming at him—like a punch to the jaw.

"What do you want?" he demanded.

Although he already knew.

"Just this. We want you to be returned to Byleukrainia—and you will be returned in spite of your sham marriage—we want you to return ready to lead. Unencumbered as you must be. You were a fighter, you know. Had very strong beliefs. You're very persuasive. You can do a lot for your country in a position of leadership."

"You mean I can do a lot for you."

"I mean your mother country. You used to have a strong allegiance to your country. You used to be an honorable man."

"Never in the way you mean it. But I was young and I did love my country—still love its people. But I don't want to go back, and if I'm forced to, it won't be to serve people like you. I want peace.''

''You are a coward if you can't fight for your country.''

Nick felt a flicker of self-doubt, but then the firmness of his beliefs gave him strength. ''Sometimes it takes more courage to be a peacemaker. To live in harmony with others.''

The caller hung up with a violent curse.

Nick stared at the phone for a very long time.

Chapter Sixteen

Toria opened the gate at her home. She looked up at the familiar white clapboard, the ornate gingerbread cutouts at the peak and porch railings, and the placid flowers that bordered the house and tumbled onto the pebble footpath. The faint glow of the fireplace shined through the living-room window, and its dusty billows of smoke puffed from the chimney.

Her house, her life. Soon to be without Nick or Anya. Back to normal. Quiet.

Maybe too quiet?

Or just quiet enough?

The front porch light blinked on and he appeared at the front door.

"I was worried you weren't coming back," he said, descending the steps to take her briefcase from her. "I made some dinner. A vegetable stew. I hope you like it. I owe you an apology."

Toria shook her head.

"I'm the one who's sorry," she said. "Here you were, defending my honor and I was ungracious about it."

"No, I insist that I apologize. I should have known that there might be extremists. I should have held my tongue when they made comments, and I certainly shouldn't have punched that man."

"No, I—"

"No, I..."

They looked at each other, with a moment of sudden understanding, an instant when they had their own joke, a private joke for themselves.

But then they laughed, both to mask uncomfortable emotions, and Nick put his arm around her as he led her into the dining room, as if it were the most natural thing in the world for them to be close.

The dining-room table was beautifully laid, with a plain white damask cloth that had been in Toria's family for years. But he had covered it with delicate red and gold leaves—their placement at once so artful and yet so seemingly random that the table looked as if it were beneath an autumn tree.

The candlelight sparkled on the gold rims of her mother's wineglasses and the plates—and Toria delighted at the napkin rings braided from willow branches. Bunches of wildflowers were arranged in low vases—pickle jars and jelly jars that had been carefully cleaned and their labels pulled off.

"Do you like it?" Nick asked shyly. "I'm not exactly Martha Stewart. You know, that lady who decorates?"

"Oh, I think Martha Stewart would be pretty jealous of you," Toria said. "You seem to be able to turn the most ordinary thing into something magical. These leaves most people would just rake into the street for pickup, and I can't imagine how you could have made the rings.''

Nick smiled with boyish delight. He held out a chair for her, and Toria playfully curtsied before she sat.

"Wait a minute," she said. "The table is only set for two. Where's Anya?"

"She got invited to Becky's for a sleep-over."

Toria felt oddly unsettled. She pushed away from her mind the memory of waking this morning entwined in Nick's arms.

"We have our interview tomorrow morning," Nick continued. "So Becky's mother agreed to drop Anya off at the INS office on her way to take Becky to school. I thought it would give us more time to prepare."

Toria swallowed hard.

"I had nearly forgotten," she said. "Or, at least, I had tried to."

"Are you still up for this?" Nick asked with forced casualness, pouring a glass of wine for her. "When you left the house this afternoon, I got the impression you wanted to wash your hands of me."

"I made you a promise," Toria said. "I always keep my promises." She bit her lip, thinking of the marriage promise itself and knew that the biggest difficulty she faced was that she really did believe her own vows.

To love him.

To honor him.

To cherish him.

Till death do you part.

Her vows hadn't said anything about being only until the INS sends the green card to Nick. Or only if he promised not to get in fights with ungentlemanly Byleukrainians. Or only if he had ideas about life that exactly coincide with her own.

Nick excused himself to the kitchen, returning with steaming bowls of stew. He whipped off a linen towel that covered a basket of warm peasant bread, and he piled her salad plate with greens.

"You're really spoiling me," Toria said.

"I should. You're my wife."

They looked up at each other. Toria thought she detected a spark of... Could it have been guilt or sheepishness on his face? She picked up her fork and focused on her salad.

The house suddenly seemed very quiet.

Quiet enough to hear the cardinal singing on the fence outside.

Quiet enough to hear the kids playing kick ball in the alley.

Quiet enough to make both of them very uncomfortable.

"I thought of you as a fast-food kind of guy," she said lightly as she tasted the delicately seasoned salad.

"You said I didn't know you very well," Nick said. "Maybe you don't know me very well, either."

"I know the names of every one of your cousins," Toria teased. "And since there's more than twenty of them, I think that's quite an accomplishment."

"Well, I know every kid who was on your high-school field-hockey team," Nick boasted. "Karen Haupt, Libby Joyce, Free Hofeld—"

"Stop!" Toria playfully put her hands on her ears.

Nick reached across the table and took her hand in his. Suddenly all the joking was over.

"You know more about me than anybody," he said.

Toria met his eyes. "You do, too," she admitted. "At least, as far as facts go."

"True. Just that far and no further," Nick said. "We're just beginning to know each other, really."

"Maybe that's how newlyweds are," Toria murmured under her breath.

"I want to know more about you," Nick continued. "I want to know your dreams and your fears, I want to know the hopes for your life that make you smile and the ones that have been crushed beneath your feet as so many young hopes are. I want to know you—and I want you to know me, as well."

Toria touched the base of her neck, reflexively trying to still her beating heart. "Why? Just to fool the INS?" she breathed.

Nick shook his head and rose from the table. He held on to her hand and led her into the living room, to the plush Turkish rug in front of the glowing fire. He sat down and pulled her down to his side. Toria felt her resistance, her natural barriers to intimacy, melting. He put his arms around her and rather than protest, she welcomed his touch, craved more, if truth were known.

Still, she faced away from him, staring into the fire, feeling his face close to hers and yet protecting her expression, fearing that her eyes might give away her true need for him.

"I have the letters," she said softly, turning to him. "They're in my briefcase."

He jerked to attention, one part wanting to pounce, to read those letters, to evaluate their worth to his cause, to study his chances. But under her gaze, he could not. He understood now how she must have recoiled inwardly when he wrote his own.

"Go on," she whispered. "You have to read them before tomorrow."

He went to her desk and opened the briefcase. She was a quick study. The envelopes were well handled and stained with fingerprints, the notes written with a variety of pens and papers, and a light rose scent came from their sheets.

"Read them," she encouraged.

He sat down at the desk and read them one at a time.

Then he stood up, gathered each note and strode quickly to the fireplace.

"No, Nick! No!" She leaped up to his arms and grabbed the letters. "Why would you do that?" she demanded.

"Because the INS has no business reading about our personal feelings."

He held her tight but her eyes skittered away from his intense stare.

"But...but...these are just make-believe."

"No, Toria, they're not, are they?"

She closed her eyes, swaying against him. "No, I guess they're not," she admitted.

"Neither were mine," he said softly.

He held her to him, tenderly kissing her hair.

"I won't lay my private feelings for my wife bare to some bureaucrat and I won't subject her to the same. We'll go in there, answer their questions and hope it is enough."

"Will it be?"

"Yes, my darling, I'm sure it will," he lied.

Nick thought about the phone call from his countrymen. He admitted to himself, for the first time, that the forces demanding his return had the upper hand. But he had something wonderful to take back to his country. The memory of his wife.

The princess of the tower, the woman he had thought beyond his reach. And yet here she was. He could have her. Just by pushing her a little further... and yet, he recoiled from the thought of manipulating her feelings. There had been enough of that in this marriage—public displays and lies.

"Fooling the INS is not the point anymore," Nick said, his sweet breath on the bare skin at her neck. "It started off that way, sure. But it's changed. It started changing the moment we made our marriage vows."

"It did?" Toria looked up at him.

"You may think that my country's customs are out of the dark ages and maybe a little bit of me is, too. I want to be a modern American man, practical and without sentimentality. But I couldn't say those words without meaning them."

"I couldn't, either," she said softly.

"Love, honor, cherish. Till death do us part."

"When I said the words, they transformed me," Toria said. "Made me into a part of you."

"Yes," Nick said. "That is it exactly."

He stared at her with liquid sapphire eyes. The fireplace popped and hissed, and Toria started, turned to watch. But Nick reached out and brought her face to his.

He kissed her.

At first his lips were as soft as suede, tentative and searching, seeking permission. Toria opened her mouth to his, wanting to throw every caution and every warning to the winds of fate. She wanted to let him in, completely into her heart.

She was nearly thirty, feeling the razor-sharp edge of life, wondering if this would be the only time for her, if this was the chance that fortune gave her, if this was the single knock of opportunity.

And yet if he had come to her when she was twenty, would she have been wise enough to see beyond the labels—primitive, hunk—to the real man?

She felt a small voice within her cry with instinctively feminine need for tenderness and gentleness. Nick pulled away, but she reached out to him tentatively. Somehow he knew of her fears. With obvious restraint, he took her into his strong arms, holding back so much force and passion that would only destroy the fragile moment.

His lips came upon hers a second time, now with more confidence at her consent. He kissed her fully, passionately—his tongue seeking each pleasure nerve within her mouth.

She shifted so that she sat astride him, and as they kissed a third time, she felt his rock-hard maleness press against her.

Suddenly, she understood the consequences of what they were doing. She hesitated. His eyes sought hers.

"I'm just so uncertain, so pulled in different directions," she said. "Where do we go from here?"

Nick shrugged thoughtfully. "I don't know," he admitted. "I don't know what I have to offer you. I don't know how far you want to take this."

"You're talking about tomorrow?" Toria said, suddenly feeling a chill.

"Yes, but only partly. We don't know if I'll be here," Nick said. "I probably won't be in America."

"Your kissing me now isn't part of making sure I'll do a good job at the interview," she teased.

Nick's eyes flashed angrily. "Of course not!" he cried out. "How can you think such a thing? Now I wish we were not married so I could prove to you that my feelings are true, that I could make love to you without your feeling betrayed or used."

"Do you want...to make love?" Toria asked breathlessly.

The question was as poignant as it was innocently suggestive. How could she know? How could she know the aching in his loins that she could provoke with her walk, with her lilting voice, with just a look?

The man on the phone had complicated things. She could be hurt—badly.

And maybe it would be better for her if he left her with memories that would fade quickly. So that she could have the things a woman needed. A husband. Children. It wouldn't happen for her if she pined for him. And he knew if they made love, she would never forget, would be faithful forever to his memory.

"I would, with all my heart, but I'm going to make you eat dinner," he said with false cheer. "I won't make love to you now. If I did, there would be a small part of you that would doubt. I will not have that. I will not let that happen."

He stood up and held his hand out to her. She looked up at him. His manhood, proud and demanding, strained against his jeans and she knew that it took every ounce of his willpower not to take her.

Funny how powerful she was, with her power being that of surrender.

She touched him.

There.

He groaned in exquisite agony, flinging his head back. He took her hand and held it away from him.

"I didn't mean to accuse you," she said. "I just meant, oh, I don't know what I meant. Maybe I'm scared."

"You should be. Of me, not the INS. Giving yourself to a man, particularly one that you've promised your life to, should always be scary. But, Toria, please don't touch me again like that, not unless we're ready. Because it takes all my strength to resist you."

She had never before thought of herself as alluring, as sexy, as seductive—only at this moment did she know, truly and deeply, and it was a precious delight.

He pulled her up to him and gently, very gently, took her arms from around his neck.

"Let's have our dinner," he said hoarsely. "Don't look at me so, sweet one. Please don't be sad."

"I'm not sad. I'm so confused. I want more. I want you."

"Darling," he said.

He saw her need, saw her confusion at the tumult within her body. He guessed that this was her first time—not in that crude calculation of whether she had ever made love, but the first time her spirit and body were united in a single hunger.

How could he leave her this way, so unfulfilled? How could he bring her to this place and then not bring her to ecstasy?

And yet, he deduced quickly, he was certain that the idea of making love was so little a part of her experience that she would have nothing available, nothing at hand, to protect herself. And he, thinking of her always as so out of reach, had nothing himself. The idea of a furtive, quick trip to the drugstore was unseemly, but the prospect of a child of his born in America, one he could not raise, was even more repugnant. He would go, but he realized that, for her, this was a sacred, fragile moment. As soon as he darted off to the all-night shop, she would look inward and regard her desires as base, juvenile and worth reconsidering. Someday she'd see making love as naturally part of their union—worth celebrating, worth joking about, worth all the soulful awe and earthly delight.

"Lie down," he commanded with a whisper.

She obeyed, lying on the rug and quivering as she watched and waited. Her amber eyes were lit with a dangerous fire and her breath came raggedly. He smoothed her hair as he would a forest animal's. She reached suddenly for his pants, but he grabbed her hand.

"Not so fast," he said. "We have time. This isn't something we're trying to get over with."

Awash in firelight, he caressed her body, tenderly taking his time at removing each piece of clothing, only losing his patience once when a delicate button at her collar resisted the efforts of his thick, clumsy-feeling fingers. When she was at last naked, she wrapped her arms around her knees in poignant modesty.

A wood nymph, he thought, remembering the legendary rulers of the thick forests of his homeland. The nymphs were known for bewitching tree-cutters and wayward shepherds.

You have certainly done that to me, Nick thought, fighting for self-control. He could take her now, quickly, demandingly, with searing passion. But that would not be right—it would frighten her and she would draw into her shell. Besides, this time was not for him. It was for her. Purely for her.

He pushed her knees apart and dipped his head to her. He knew it wouldn't last long—she was so close, so ready. She groaned as he touched the rosebud core of her womanhood. She tasted of honey and milk.

"Nick," she warned.

With his palm on her pubic mound, he felt the sudden first contractions. She arched to meet him, strained, each muscle of her body clenched, and then she tumbled down, down, down. She closed her eyes, a bright red flush on her chest subsided, and a womanly feline smile told him he had given her pleasure.

He reached to the couch for the antique quilt to warm her.

"What about...?" she asked, touching him on his thigh.

He knew that for her the very action was boldness itself. He didn't want to rebuff it, and yet if she left her hand there, he would lose control.

"Darling, no," he said. "Your pleasure is enough for me right now."

She looked entirely confused—and then that confusion transformed to hurt. She wouldn't say it, but he knew.

"Toria, I cannot leave a child here," he said. "We don't know what will happen tomorrow. I cannot leave a child that I can't raise."

"But what if we win? What if you get to stay?"

"Then I will make love to you every night. Every afternoon in your office. Every morning in my lab. I'll make love to you and give you children. Many, many children."

"And if we don't?"

"I won't leave a child here."

He didn't mean to be so harsh, but there was no other way. That was the reality—they could be torn apart tomorrow. In fact, it was likely they would be.

"Can't I do what you did to me?"

Nick swallowed a groan of pleasure. A tormenting pleasure. One that he knew had to be denied.

"Have you ever?"

"No. Never before. I'd like to. Really, I would."

He was too ready, too intense, too hard. One touch from her, one kiss at just the right spot, and he'd be gone. He couldn't be sure he'd have his control. He would seem like an animal to her. He shook his head.

"Darling, this was enough," he choked.

"But you didn't..."

"No, this is enough. Just have dinner with me. Let us enjoy tonight. The sun will rise tomorrow—tomorrow will happen without our having to do anything about it tonight. And if we can come together tomorrow night, my love, I will never leave you. I will show you every way there is to make love."

"You want me now."

Nick laughed heartily at her bluntly innocent words. "My sweet one, I have wanted to make love to you since I first saw you," he said. "Standing apart from the others in the courtyard of the dean's house."

"Did you really? You weren't lying when you told that story at the reception?"

Nick shook his head. "I was never lying about that." He took her hand and kissed the palm. "That is where my heart is now," he said.

She dressed and he watched her in melancholy silence. Then he led her back into the dining room. They ate, and the food was remarkable—tastes were more vivid, textures accentuated. And yet food did not satisfy.

When their plates were empty, Toria felt like a gambler, felt like throwing her cards on the table, rolling the dice for one night of passion like no other. Even if the tomorrows wouldn't come, she wanted hers tonight.

"Come on," Nick said, licking his fingers and pressing them against the flames of the candles to put them out. "Leave the plates. I'll wash them later."

"Where are we going?" Toria asked breathlessly, as he grabbed her hand and pulled her toward the stairs.

"I want you to know me, really know me," Nick said. "I want you to see the part of me that is really what I'm about."

"All right," Toria answered tremulously.

She followed him upstairs, to the guest room. He flicked on the light and opened the closet. Her eyes blinking to adjust to the bright light, she sat down on the bed.

He pulled out two pairs of hip boots and a flashlight on a shoulder strap.

"What are those for?" she asked, recoiling.

"I want you to come to the river with me," he said, puzzled as she suddenly burst into laughter. "I want you to see the world I love."

Chapter Seventeen

"Those are the native violets," Nick said, shoving his flashlight deep into the bushes at the water's edge. He pulled branches apart so that Toria could see the fragile blooms.

"Smell them. So beautiful. They're Illinois' state flower—and they also grow in other parts of the world. Even my mother country. But not too many grow in Naperville because they're so fragile. The sun can scorch them. Pollution can wither their leaves. These are the last blooms, summer's last voluptuous moment."

Toria crouched next to him on the muddy bank, holding on to Nick's arm to keep from slipping.

"They're so beautiful," she said. "But no one would know they were there."

They were far from the Riverwalk, Naperville's paved and cultivated park along the river. They had started there, among the cultivated geraniums and the potted chrysanthemums, and then had hiked west, quickly leaving the streetlights and comfortably clustered houses behind.

He knew every inch of the trail, every flower, every King Rail's nest, every gray squirrel's lair. As he trod quietly along the wooded embankment, he pointed them out—shining his flashlight only when absolutely necessary, not wanting to frighten his quarry.

When he led her into the water, he avoided the eddies and undertows—knowing the river's contours as well as he did the paths on land.

Toria at first struggled with every step, finding the wading boots ungainly and heavy, blinking against the dark, shivering in Nick's heavy quilted vest.

He flipped off the flashlight. "Look," he said, pointing out the Eastern sky. "It's already dawn."

"We've been out here for six hours?" Toria asked incredulously.

Nick nodded.

"Want to stop by McDonald's on the way back? It might be my last American meal."

Toria wanted to laugh at his request, and then she stilled. Her heart galloped and she reached out to take his hand. "I'm scared," she admitted.

"I am, too," he said gruffly. "But I am only scared that I will fail you somehow."

Toria thought ruefully that only she could do that.

"SO LET ME get this straight, Mrs. Sankovitch," Agent Rogers said, putting particular emphasis on the word *Mrs*.

Toria rubbed her temples and stretched in the metal folding chair she had been perched in for over two hours.

"Mrs. Sankovitch?" Agent Smith prompted more neutrally. He sat to her left, scribbling notes.

"I'm sorry. I'm paying attention," Toria said. "But I'm just a little tired."

"The interview is almost over," Agent Rogers snapped.

"We hope you understand we're just doing our job," Smith said. He was more pleasant than Agent Rogers—at the beginning of the interview, he had fixed her a cup of tea and had nodded and smiled often during the session. He had even mentioned that he went to North Central College himself a long time ago, but that he'd never taken any of her parents' classes, though he had seen them around campus a lot.

"Mrs. Sankovitch, we're going to review again that first interaction between yourself and Dr. Sankovitch," Agent Rogers said, leafing through her notes.

Smith and Toria sat up straight and paid attention.

"You say that you met at the dean's party," Rogers said.

"Yes," Toria agreed. "In the courtyard."

"And Nick asked you out immediately after?"

"Yes. I thought we already went over this."

"We did," Rogers said. "I just wanted to be sure I understood you correctly."

She pulled a black box from her desk and slipped out a videotape.

"Especially in light of this," she said, pushing the videotape into the VCR behind her desk. She flipped on the television, and Anya, sticking her tongue out at the camera, appeared on the screen. She was wearing a cowboy hat. The camera zoomed in to the face of the woman reporter in the tomato red suit.

Toria felt her mouth go dry as Anya giggled and pranced around, describing the music box in Toria's office and how she had brought Toria and her father together.

DOWN THE HALL, Nick leaned backward, getting the kinks out of his neck. He wasn't used to sitting this long—maybe that was why he found meetings a waste of time, he mused. Besides, the metal folding chair was far too small for his frame, and he felt as if he was on a doll's chair. He picked up his soda can and reminded himself that he had finished his drink nearly an hour before. And it didn't look as if these agents were going to give him another chance to go to the vending machines. But he did want to check on Anya.

"Your daughter is fine," the dark-haired agent with the red tie said, without looking up from his papers. "She's being watched in the reception area."

The other agent turned the page on his legal pad and stared at Nick with a thoughtful expression.

"Ready to continue, Dr. Sankovitch?"

"Yes."

"Let's review some of the qualities that first attracted you to your wife. Can you tell us a little about that?"

Nick took a deep breath.

"She's beautiful and intelligent, obviously," he said, hearing the scratching of the agents' pencils on their notepads but no longer bothered by it. "And very kind. Very good with Anya. But I think what I love most about her, what I saw from the beginning is that she is like a beautiful native violet with delicate leaves and petals that are swollen with color. Her kind of delicate beauty cannot survive without taller plants, sturdier plants protecting the violet's leaves from direct sunlight and I found myself feeling..."

The agents stared at him openmouthed and dumbfounded.

"Can't you understand that I love her?" Nick asked. "I really do love her. There shouldn't be any other question. I made my vows and they are permanent to me."

"We were thinking more along the lines of shared hobbies," one said. "You know, like stamp collecting or square dancing."

Nick shrugged.

"Hobbies? We both enjoy late-night car rides and getting milk shakes from the drive-through. We both like reruns, and I'm starting to understand opera. We both like working in the garden and oh, yes, we both like rodeos."

An efficient-looking young woman in a navy suit entered and placed a small white note card in front of the agent. He read it and a weary smile broke out on his face.

"Ah, speaking of rodeos," he said, and reached into his desk drawer for a black box. "We'd like you to take a look at this."

As the first flickering images of his daughter appeared on the screen, Nick knew he was finished.

"I'M SORRY," Toria said tearfully.

"I hate you. You lied to me," Anya said with the kind of venom that only a very hurt child can have. "You said it was forever. You said you two were really married."

"I know," Toria said. "We wanted it to be that way. But we both did what we did for you. I wanted to help."

"I don't need that kind of help," Anya snapped. "You could have told me the truth. At least I could have known what was going on."

"We thought it was better this way."

"I thought it was better," Nick corrected, crouching to be near them. "I was the one who insisted that you not be told."

Toria and Nick looked at each other, wanting to hug each other, to comfort each other, to apologize, to ask about the future, to mourn what could have been. But Anya had been sitting on the floor of the INS reception area all morning. And only now did she know what had been kept from her.

"Then you were the one who lied to me," Anya repeated darkly to her father. "I hate you, too."

"I wanted to give you a chance to live in America," Nick said.

"Don't bother," Anya lashed out. She picked up her Barbie dolls and stood up. "I thought you were in love."

"We—"

Toria and Nick looked at each other.

"I don't have anything to offer you," he said, holding up his cuffed hands. "It's regulations."

Agent Smith, who had been standing a few discreet paces behind, walked over.

"Dr. Sankovitch, we will be driving you back into Chicago for processing before your flight to Byleukrainia," he said. "We will stop at your house and you will have ten minutes to pack anything you wish to take with you."

Agent Rogers, her high heels clicking efficiently on the linoleum floors, came out to the reception area.

"We'd better hurry," she said briskly. "His flight is at ten tonight. And Chicago will have a lot of paperwork to complete before then."

Toria reached out to give Anya a hug, but the little girl slipped out of her arms.

WITH A WEARY HEART, Toria drove the pickup to the house, leading the nondescript white Chevy in which the agents, Nick and Anya were riding.

At the house, she sat tight-lipped in the hall while Agent Rogers helped Anya assemble her Barbie doll collection. Agent Smith followed Nick, carrying his suitcase.

Toria's heart broke at the sight of her husband in handcuffs.

"Can't you take them off?" she asked Smith.

Smith shook his head. "Regulations," he said.

Toria looked down at her hands and took off her wedding ring, the ring that had been in Nick's family for so long. She would have liked to keep it as a remembrance of him, but as her eyes drifted toward the window and the light, she knew she'd have something else. The garden where the tulips he had so

carefully nurtured would bloom—again and again.
The Riverwalk where secret paths and hollows lay
undisturbed, the violets that no one else noticed under the brush, the scent of him that would never quite
leave her house would be hers alone. Those were the
important yet subtle reminders for memories that
would never dim.

And, of course, there was a television set.

He would find someone, making his life—however difficult—in Byleukrainia more livable. He deserved to make that life with someone else to give
Anya a home. Someone else to listen to him, to hold
his hand. Someone else to sleep next to him and have
his children. She wouldn't ask him to put his—and
Anya's—life on hold.

Her heart breaking, she looked one last time at her
wedding ring. "Here," she said, putting the ring in
Nick's shirt pocket.

His eyes widened, and he looked as if he might
protest. But with a shudder, he nodded and turned his
head away.

In five minutes—the Barbie dolls assembled and
packed—the Sankovitches left.

Anya barely suffered a hug from Toria.

Nick kissed Toria gently on the cheek but said
nothing.

Agent Smith shrugged goodbye.

And Agent Rogers informed her that Toria would
not be prosecuted because Nick had consented to im-
mediate deportation and had given up his right to
appeal.

Toria stood on the porch and watched the white Chevy until it turned the corner at Locust Street and was gone.

The house seemed unbearably large, quiet, empty as she closed the door.

And so did her heart.

SHE WENT to the office to work.

What else was there to do?

Bewitched made her cry—thinking of how much Nick and Anya loved that show. And when she found herself humming the theme music like a funeral dirge, she knew she'd better find something else to do.

Reading in bed was worse—the upstairs smelled of Anya's bubble gum and Nick's citrus-fresh masculine scent.

Going to sleep was impossible, because when she pulled her staid cotton nightgown from the drawer, all she could think of was Nick reading *Sophisticated Woman* and trying to figure out what kind of nightgowns she would wear.

Sitting in the guest room and finding one of his shirts was torture, holding it against her like touching fire.

So she packed her briefcase and headed for the campus.

It was midafternoon and there were many people on the quad. Though she said hello to everyone who greeted her, there was no question that she wanted to be left alone.

She tried to grade exams, but eventually set them aside. Then she tried to read a paper a colleague had sent to her for comments. She made tea and didn't drink it.

Finally, Toria found the only thing she could do— sit in the chair at the window and play the music box. Over and over. She wanted to mourn. He had been her cavalry officer. She had been his lady. And now there was only one place where they would dance.

The knock on the door at three o'clock startled her, but she kept quiet, pulling inside herself. She wasn't ready to help somebody with homework or listen to a colleague's discovery of some obscure writer.

The knock again.

She held her breath. Maybe they would go away.

And then she heard it.

Her name said once. Just once. So softly. In that familiar voice that she loved.

Chapter Eighteen

"How did you get here?" Toria whispered, shutting the door behind him with a quick glance to reassure herself that nobody was watching.

"Agent Rogers had some kind of emergency back at the office," Nick explained. "I persuaded Smith to take Anya to the ice-cream shop. We've got an hour. He will say we hit heavy traffic on the way to Chicago."

"Why are you here?"

"Only this," he said, and pulled from inside his shirt a handful of violets. Crushed, wilted, faded, but still beautiful. She took them in her hand and smelled their last moment of scent.

"I need you to know that I love you," Nick said. "I love you with all my heart. Someday I want to come back, not just because of Anya or because of my work—but because I love you. Really love you."

He pulled the ring out of his pocket and put it on her finger.

"Please take this back," he begged.

"So you still want me as your wife? Even if…there is no keeping you here?"

"Always in my heart this is so," he answered. "You are my wife. Maybe it began as an arrangement, but the love I felt for you from a distance long ago has grown now to the love a man feels only once. And I am not so Americanized, you see, that I can walk away from my sacred vows and from the love of my life."

Though her heart soared, she still saw reason. "Nick, you must think of Anya. You need a mother for her."

"We will manage. But you... perhaps you need a husband, a finer one, a husband who is home for you, who will make love to you every night, who will give you children and who will raise those children with you. You should have those things. And you should be practical."

"Nick, Americans may be practical, but they're also very romantic and very devoted to their families. I love you, I made my vows and you are my only husband. I want no other."

"We may never see each other again."

"Then let me come with you," Toria begged impulsively.

"To Byleukrainia? No, never. It's too unstable, too dangerous. Life would be too hard." He left out any mention of the menacing phone call making clear she was unwelcome.

"I could do it."

"You could, I know, because you are brave and good. But no." He shook his head. "Live the life you deserve here. Find a man. Make a life. I will not blame you for that."

"But, Nick, I don't want another husband. I don't want another man's children. I want you. Those vows we made to each other, they mean nothing if we can't wait for each other." She took his hand, wincing at the marks left by the cuffs. She silently thanked Agent Smith, who no doubt was the one who had taken them off. She kissed his palm, lingering at the calluses. "That is where my heart is," she said, looking up at him. "I can't give myself to another man. It would be as if a loyal knight deserted the tsarina."

He remembered the tales he had told her. Of fidelity and devotion unto death. Not unlike the marriage vows.

It was then he marveled at his wife.

Practical, yes.

Modern, without a doubt.

Refined, but of course.

And his lover for eternity?

He caressed her face with his palm. "Then that means I must come back soon," he said. "Somehow I must come back. If only in my dreams." He kissed her, his lips memorizing every nuance of her mouth, of her velvet tongue, of her cool breath. "We have so little time," he sighed. "I wish that I could give you a canopied wedding bed and cover the sheets with rose petals. It is a custom, you know."

She took the violets he gave her, nearly crushed in his hand, and threw them on the couch.

"Here is our wedding bed and our night will have to be a stolen hour," she said.

"Are you sure?"

"Yes," she replied with a nod.

She had never been more sure of anything.

"Might be a little risqué," he said, giving her a half smile.

She remembered how they had argued about when their first lovemaking would have been. "Why else would I marry you?" she quipped. "If I wanted bland and boring, I could have married someone else."

He pulled out a small package from his pocket. "I stopped at the drugstore," he said. "I hoped that you would want to make love to me."

"No children?"

"No children until I can be their father," he said. He didn't tell her that the most painful possibility—that of a child he would never see, a child who would call another man Daddy—haunted him.

While he checked the lock on her door, she took off her dress and slipped off her shoes. He watched her, briefly closing his eyes to gain control over his emotions as she pulled off her bra and panties. She started to cover herself with her hands, her natural modesty making him smile.

"No, don't," he said. "I have to carry this picture of you with me for a long time. Let me see you. All of you."

She hesitated and then, her hands ungainly at her sides, leaned back on the couch.

He approached, unstrapping his belt, unbuttoning his shirt. She swallowed. He threw his shirt on the desk and kicked off his boots. He unzipped his pants and pushed them to the ground.

Then he stood before her.

Proud. Manly. Hard.

Her husband.

At first, she looked away, her eyes skittering around the room. But he didn't move, demanding silently that she look at him, that she memorize his body for the coming time apart. She had never looked at a man, really looked at a man, before—her few encounters being largely in darkness, furtive, maybe even a little clumsy. All with an atmosphere that had allowed her a shield against true intimacy.

But there was nothing for her to hide behind now.

This was not the time or place for sudden modesty.

Her eyes met his steady, deep gaze. And then she looked at him, drinking in every contour of his body, enjoying every defined muscle, lingering at his rigid abdomen. Then her gaze went farther down and she felt her sex respond.

And just as she was ready to beg him to come to her, he did, as if knowing her every thought and feeling.

He knelt beside her and kissed her first on her stomach, then laid his head gently there. "I will remember this," he said. "This is where I promise you, someday, I will give you a child of our own making."

They smiled as they thought of Anya.

Their Anya.

And the possibility of another child.

He put the sheath on him.

Then their thoughts and feelings returned to the present, to their senses and their longing for remembrance. He kissed her on the patch of hair between her legs. As they fluttered apart, he teased the bud within.

"Oh, please no, Nick!"

He stopped abruptly, raising his head. "Have I hurt you?" he asked.

"No, it's not that," she said, caressing his cheek. "It's just…it's just…I want you inside me when I…"

"Oh," he said, smiling. "Then I will make you ready. But of course not too ready."

And he did, bringing her to the brink but expertly taking her back. Again and again, until she thought she would cry out.

When she thought she could bear no more pleasure, he stopped. And came over her, easing between her legs, stretching himself the full length of their wedding bed, his manhood poised on top of her.

"I will come back," Nick said, his eyes searching hers. "I don't care how long it takes or what I have to do, but I will be back."

"I know," Toria said, putting her hand over his mouth. "You'll come back."

"I will," he promised again as he entered her. "I will be back for you."

His eyes closed in pleasure, and he had to stop so that he wouldn't peak too early. But the first caresses of her orgasm teased him, eventually tipping him over the edge of the precipice of control.

"Oh, my love," he gasped as the last shudder of his passion was spent. "I will be back. With every ounce of my strength, with every day of my life, I will fight for that."

LATER, AFTER AN HOUR that had moved more quickly than any other she had known, she watched from behind the lace curtains on the window. Nick walked across the quad and a man approached him.

Toria's heart fluttered just a little—it was the man who had been watching them. At their wedding. Outside the house. At the rodeo.

INS, no doubt about it. He must have been watching them constantly. No wonder the agents had been able to so quickly uncover the truth.

But what was the truth?

Sure, it had been an arranged marriage. A marriage of convenience. Meant for deceit.

Now it was everything.

Toria shivered and pulled her dress up to warm her. Nick started to walk away with the man, turning once to wave at the window.

She waved back but couldn't tell if he even saw her.

TORIA WAS EATING double-fudge ice cream directly from the carton when the knock came.

Agents Smith and Rogers stood on her porch.

"Yes?" she asked coolly.

The agents looked at her attire—jeans and one of Nick's shirts. Bunny slippers on her feet.

She had found the UPS package containing her trousseau on the front porch when she had gotten home. She had decided not to open it until Nick returned, perhaps in years. But a trousseau could wait as long as her heart.

Until then, his shirts.

"We know it's late," Rogers said. "But Agent Smith here lost Dr. Sankovitch. We thought he might be here."

Toria opened her mouth, started to say something and then saw Smith's sheepish frown. He looked so guilty. And she was so grateful to him for the hour she had had with Nick.

"When did you lose him?" she asked neutrally, beginning to worry for her husband.

"When he came to see you. He never came back."

"Anya's in the car," Rogers said. "We're here to search the house. You can either allow us to do so voluntarily or not."

"Come on in," Toria said, shrugging. "Why don't you let Anya in, too? It's a little chilly outside."

"I'll go get her," Smith said.

Toria shuffled back into the living room and sat down on the couch.

"Isn't that *Gilligan's Island*?" Rogers asked.

"Yes, it is."

"Isn't that Dr. Sankovitch's favorite?"

"Yes, it's my husband's favorite."

"I thought you didn't watch television," Rogers said.

Toria looked at the woman, trying to remember that she was just doing her job.

Still...

"I've been watching television ever since I got married," she said and stared at the set.

A very sullen Anya came in and sat on the couch.

"I'm still mad at you," she said. "And I'll be mad at you forever. Just so you know. Even if you guys are married for love now that marrying for immigration hasn't worked. I'm mad, Toria."

"That's okay," Toria said, although it really wasn't. Oh, how her heart broke at the sight of her Anya. But she knew that whatever pain she felt, it was infinitely worse for the little girl. "I think your feelings will change someday. I hope they do, anyway."

"Can I still keep the tea set?"

"Of course you can. When I give you something, it's forever."

The agents searched through the house. Toria could hear them upstairs.

"I want you to know I love you and your father," Toria said softly. "It's just that I didn't love your father at first. We lied about that and I'm sorry. We thought we were doing the right thing."

"I know," Anya said, her eyes filling with tears. "It's just, well, maybe I'm so mad because I'm going to miss everything. You. This house. My school. My friend Becky. Even Michael—and you know I don't like him ever since he had a birthday party and didn't invite me."

"Oh, I know, Anya. I'm going to miss you, too."

Toria pulled Anya into her arms just as Anya burst into sobs.

A SHORT TIME LATER, Rogers and Smith gave up.

"Why don't you tell us about the last time you saw Dr. Sankovitch?" Rogers asked.

Toria blushed.

"All right, don't tell us about that," Smith said quickly. "Just tell us about him leaving."

"He went with one of your guys."

"What do you mean?" Smith said. "He was supposed to meet me at the ice-cream shop."

"No, he went with the other one," Toria insisted. "The bald one. He met Nick at the end of the quad."

"What other one?" Rogers demanded.

"Your other agent. The one who has been following us. He was lurking around at our wedding, kept his car outside our house, even shadowed us at the rodeo."

The two agents looked at each other.

"We haven't had an agent following you," Rogers said carefully.

"Then who was he?" Anya asked.

"That's what we'd like to know," Rogers said softly, for the first time showing a human face.

Just then the phone rang.

Chapter Nineteen

"If you want to see him again, don't say anything—just listen."

She didn't say a word.

Him.

Somebody had him.

Toria gripped the phone and looked up at the expectant faces around her.

"Anyone there with you?" The gravelly voice demanded.

"Yes. Yes, there is," Toria replied with false gaiety.

"Tell them I'm your sister. From Miami," the voice ordered and then laughed, a harsh grating cough of evil humor. "From Miami. That's pretty good. A sister from Miami."

"Who is it?" Agent Rogers whispered.

"My sister," Toria said. "From Miami."

"I didn't know you had a sister in Miami," Anya said.

"I just didn't tell you about her," Toria said. "It's Joy. My younger sister. She lives there."

"Good job," the voice on the phone encouraged. "Now I'll tell you what you have to do. Do you remember the restaurant where you went yesterday?"

How could she forget? She thought of the men and their anger. Had they taken Nick?

"Yes, Joy, I remember," she said.

"Go there. Only you. If we see anyone else, you'll be sorry."

"How...how do I know...Joy?"

"I'll put him on."

She heard movement, and then—as if from a distance, she heard a scuffling, somebody coughing, a chair shifting and yet, barely there—"Toria, I love you. Don't—"

And then nothing. Toria thought she had been cut off, but she kept her face as blank as possible.

And waited.

Agent Rogers and Smith stared openly.

Anya shrugged and sat back to continue watching TV.

"Aunt Joy" came back on the line.

"Remember, Professor, no one comes with you. Now say goodbye like a good big sister."

Toria shivered. "Goodbye, Joy, I'll talk to you later," she said, and put the receiver back on the telephone.

She looked up at the two agents.

"What are you going to do now?" Agent Rogers asked her coolly.

At first Toria thought her phone call had been overheard, but looking into the agent's face, she knew they hadn't heard a thing. She almost took them into her confidence but then remembered the harsh voice and the threat. Besides, these two were only interested in one thing—getting her husband out of the country.

"I was going to watch some TV," Toria explained in as natural a voice as she could muster. "And call my sister back. We couldn't really talk with you around." She stared brazenly at the agents, who maybe would have the good sense to take the hint.

"We're sorry to have disturbed you," Agent Rogers said. "The only reason I'm asking is that we don't know what to do with Anya while we try to locate her father. We could call social services and see if they have a bed somewhere..."

As her voice trailed off, Anya came to stand next to Toria.

"What my boss is trying to say is that we screwed up," Smith said. "And having to bring in social services is only going to make this worse."

"Correction," Rogers said. "You screwed up."

Smith nodded good-naturedly. "What she's saying is that I screwed up. If we can find Nick and find him quickly, I might have a job tomorrow. But if we call social services, the whole thing's going to burst wide open."

"Couldn't I stay here, please?" Anya begged. "I promise I'll be good. Even if I am mad at you."

As Toria hesitated, Rogers and Smith pounced. They declared it to be a wonderful idea. Toria inwardly groaned—she would ordinarily have been delighted, but she had to get to that restaurant. By herself.

Then she noticed Anya's friendship bracelet. Becky! She could drop Anya off there, persuade Becky's mom to keep her for a while and drive to Chicago.

"I'd be delighted," Toria announced. "I promise she'll be fine here—and, even if you screwed up, Mr. Smith, I am very grateful to you."

After awkward goodbyes, Toria shut the door behind the agents.

"Come on," she said to Anya, flipping off the television.

"Where are we going?"

"You're spending the night with Becky again," Toria said, gathering up her keys and purse and shoving her feet into the sneakers by the front door.

"You don't want me around?"

"Of course that's not it," Toria answered, giving Anya a quick hug. "It's because I think I might know where your father is."

"So let me go with you!"

"No, it . . . it would keep you up too late," Toria answered lamely, not wanting to alarm Anya and yet not very good at excuses.

"I want to go," Anya insisted.

"WHO IS BECKY and why should I care that she has the measles?" Missy asked, pulling her red silk robe a little more tightly around herself as she stood in the doorway of her town house.

Toria took a deep breath, reminding herself that only calm, careful action now would do Nick any good.

"I have to go somewhere, and you have to take care of Anya for me."

"How about tomorrow night on the sleep-over?" Missy suggested.

"Now. Right now, Missy," Toria said, handing Missy the Barbie-doll suitcase and leading Anya past Missy into the front foyer.

"What's gotten into you?" Missy asked, staring with utterly horrified fascination at the little suitcase. "I mean, you're not known for being really pushy. In fact, if anyone else did this I would be livid. All you're doing is making me curious."

"I have to do something very important, dangerous even, and I can't have Anya with me," Toria whispered.

"Darling, the closest thing you've ever done to dangerous was put on your jammies, pour a cup of hot cocoa and watch 'Murder, She Wrote.'"

"This is more serious than that," Toria said, leaning to Missy's shoulder and trying not to sneeze at the heavy Chanel No 5 perfume. "Nick's in trouble."

"And you're going to help him?" Missy asked in disbelief.

"Yes."

"This is more serious than I ever thought."

Missy stepped over to the bottom of the spiral staircase.

"George!" she screamed.

A man, hunk material from what Toria could see, appeared at the top of the stairs. Bare chested. The top button of his jeans undone. His hair falling forward over his chiseled face.

"Playdate's over," Missy purred. "Go home, George. You can come back tomorrow."

"Huh?"

"I've got a sleep-over," Missy explained, putting one arm around Anya. "We're playing Barbies. It's a girl thing. You're not invited. Get your shirt on and go home."

As George disappeared into the bedroom, grumbling mightily, Missy wagged her finger in Toria's face.

"This better be really important, girlfriend, because George might not be Mr. Right, but he was Mr. January in the this year's Firemen of DuPage County calendar."

AN HOUR LATER, Toria had survived three sets of no-commercial-interruption Van Halen. The music helped her concentrate on the driving and not the dangers Nick—and she—faced.

Her legs felt wobbly, she discovered, as she got out of the pickup on the dark, rain-soaked street downtown. Her chest hurt from hyperventilating.

She hoped she'd arrived in time.

She looked up and down the deserted street and, with a quick prayer for courage, walked across to the storefront door. A fan above the door leaked into a puddle, splattering her socks. She pushed at the door, nothing happened. And so, she knocked.

"Who is it?" someone demanded from inside.

"It's Toria Sankovitch," she said, surprising herself at the use of her married name. And with the undercurrent of courage that she had never known she had. "I've come to get my husband," she added more boldly.

With a click of the deadbolt, the door opening only so much, an angular, bearded face stared at her.

"Alone?"

Toria nodded, recoiling from the hostility emanating from the man, as surely as the smell of stale sweat and cheap after-shave.

"Get in here!" the man ordered, shoving open the door and grabbing Toria's arm.

Like a terrified Alice in Wonderland, Toria tumbled into the restaurant that had once seemed quaint. The rustic chairs and tables had been shoved up against one wall and the tinkling folk music was gone. She blinked, adjusting her eyes to the darkness—a single light bulb hung from the ceiling. Seven—no, eight—men stood in a ring just outside the circle of light, their faces menacingly shadowed.

Her stomach turned as she saw Nick tied up to a chair, his face dripping with sweat, his shirt ripped, an angry bruise on his temple.

"Nick!" she cried out, running to him—only to be stopped by a strong hand.

Then she saw another face—a man sitting on an armchair next to a small side table, a cup of Turkish coffee and a pack of Sobranie cigarettes available to him.

The bald man, the one who had been tailing them.

He certainly wasn't INS.

If he wasn't INS, who was he?

"You made a mistake, darling," Nick chided, with as casual an attitude as if he were simply dining with friends. "You should have stayed home."

Toria shook her head. "I couldn't do that."

One of the men held out a white scarf to her. She recoiled.

"Take it," the bald man ordered. "Cover your hair."

Toria stared at him. "No," she said firmly, bracing herself for whatever would come next.

But the bald man merely shrugged to the men who encircled them, as if to say, What did we expect?

"She's here," he said to Nick. "Say it."

Nick shook his head. "I won't."

The bald man sighed and drank from his coffee cup. Then he began talking in a language Toria couldn't understand, quietly at first but with considerable emotion as his voice grew more forceful.

"What is he saying?" Toria demanded.

"He's telling your husband to divorce you because you are an American," a voice at Toria's shoulder said.

Toria broke her gaze at her husband long enough to look around into dark kohl-rimmed eyes.

"You!" Toria whispered sharply. "I wanted to thank you for having opened the door for us before..."

"Shhh! Just turn around. Listen."

Toria didn't have to be told twice. Her husband was all that mattered to her now. She watched as the bald man continued to talk—at once pleading and cajoling, then threatening and vulgar.

"All he has to do is say 'I divorce you' three times and everyone will be made happy," the woman explained. "That's the Byleukrainian custom. If he is being deported back to our country, they don't want him to be disgraced by a marriage tie to an American."

"Disgraced?"

"They want him to be a figurehead, a symbol of their brand of patriotism. Can't do that with an American wife."

"But we can't get divorced. We love each other."

"This was a marriage arranged to circumvent immigration laws," the woman scoffed. "Wasn't it?"

"It started off that way," Toria admitted, thinking it odd that this woman, who looked right out of the past century with her modest, dark headscarf would talk as though she were a very up-to-date lawyer. "It started that way, but now it's different. Our marriage is a real marriage. We love each other."

Nick spat out what sounded to be a surly Byleukrainian curse. Whatever he said only made the bald man more angry.

"Nick, just do it!" Toria pleaded. "Say the words."

The bald man started. Nick looked over at Toria.

"Do it?" he asked. "Is that what our marriage means to you?"

"What are your choices?" she asked. "Say the magic words three times and we get out of here or keep refusing and they'll...?" She stared uneasily at the gun one of the men held.

"Those aren't my choices," Nick said. "If I divorce you, even just this way, I've renounced our marriage, I've turned my back on you. We can't just shrug it off because we don't agree with the custom. It's our marriage. It meant more to us than a bunch of 'I do's'—we made a sacred vow. I don't want to say the words because I don't want to disgrace my marriage promises."

"You're just being proud."

"I'm just being honorable."

"I thought honorable simply meant surviving."

"Maybe I meant something more. Real honor. I have to leave you. Do I go as your husband, or do I go as your ex?"

"I want you to stay alive."

"Does that mean you want a divorce? Does this mean these extremists get their way because they stomp their feet and threaten to hold their breath until we get divorced?"

"Aren't they threatening something a little more serious?"

"Just answer the question. Do you want this divorce?"

Toria started to say yes, do it, please, do anything these crazy men want. But as her eyes met his, she knew how much her marriage really meant to her.

Maybe I'm crazy, she thought. But if she loved him, she needed to respect him, as well.

Reluctantly, torn up inside, she shook her head.

"Then stand by me and I'll stand by you," Nick said.

Toria swallowed the hardness in her throat. The bald man pulled a small silver gun from a shoulder holster beneath his jacket. He stood up, said a few words in Byleukrainian to Nick and looked around at his followers.

"Nick, maybe we're making a mistake," Toria said, fighting to keep herself from screaming.

"Just take care of Anya," he said calmly. "Be her mother and her father."

"Always," Toria promised.

The man entreated him one more time, alternating between a guttural order and a soothing request.

Toria closed her eyes.

"I think we've got enough on them," the woman at her shoulder said.

Toria turned without taking her eyes off Nick.

"Are you talking to me?" she asked, and then something caught her eye. "Or to that—oh, my, is that a microphone attached to your scarf?"

"Toria!" Nick screamed.

Toria's instincts took over and she threw herself to the ground, crawling beneath a table.

She looked up at the woman, who had ripped off her head scarf and torn away her robes to reveal jeans and a simple blouse. She held a gun trained on the bald man, and with a jerk of her head, the men around the restaurant dropped their guns.

She said something, her tone harsh and mocking, in Byleukrainian.

Nick laughed heartily, as deeply as he had when he had first heard Toria's proposal of marriage. His solitary laughter echoed through the restaurant.

How could he laugh at a time like this? Toria wondered.

"What did she say?" Toria demanded. "What's so funny?"

"She said never underestimate the power of a woman."

Just then the doors to the restaurant burst open and the room was flooded with officers.

Chapter Twenty

"I re-read the file in the car," Agent Rogers said, smoothing her suit jacket over her shoulder holster. "You're an only child. You don't have a sister in Miami. Besides, you're a terrible liar. That's been your problem from the start."

For once, Agent Rogers's uptight efficiency didn't annoy.

In fact, it was downright lovable, Toria thought. She decided that she really liked Agent Rogers.

And she especially liked Agent Tarini Schaskyla-vitch of the Byleukrainian Special Forces. Liked her ability to use a gun. Liked her sense of humor. If many Byleukrainian women were like her, the country would soon get past its time of troubles.

"I'm glad you guys found us," Toria whispered.

"Just doing our job," Rogers replied with a sniff. "Agent Schaskylavitch tipped us off that the extremists were squeezing new immigrants and funneling money to continue the war back home. She discovered the plot to get Nick here to be a front for their political aims. Tarini goes the extra mile on work like this—she's a real professional."

"I'm just grateful we're alive."

"We are too, Mrs. Sankovitch."

Toria looked over at Nick, his forehead being swabbed by Smith, who had brought a first-aid kit in from the car. Then she did a double take. "Did you say Mrs. Sankovitch?"

Rogers bit her lip. "Yeah, I guess I did," she said, wrinkling her nose.

"Thanks."

"For calling you Mrs. Sankovitch?"

"Thanks for everything. I'm very grateful." Grateful to Rogers, her partner Smith, and Agent Schaskylavitch—as well as the dozens of police, INS agents and FBI agents who had descended on the restaurant at their command. Schaskylavitch had saved Nick's life, blowing her cover just as the leader of this fundamentalist group was ready to...

Toria didn't even want to think about how close they had come.

It didn't matter now. The men had been taken away. Agent Rogers was already complaining about the mountain of paperwork that would be necessary to complete for their deportation.

Toria crouched down in front of Nick, taking the cotton from Smith and wiping away the dried blood from her husband's forehead. "You're really going to have a bump tomorrow," she said.

"I know, but you'll never see it," Nick said ruefully. "They're about to take me in. They still think they can get me on that plane to Byleukrainia."

"Oh, Nick, I wish..."

"Don't wish anything. If we are meant to be together, it will all happen soon enough. All that's important to me is that we love each other, we're married and we will see it through. There is nothing more to wish for—and so many people have less." He took her hand and kissed the palm, lingering over the sweet, pale flesh. "There is where my heart is, while I may be a world away."

Toria bit back her tears.

Agents Smith and Rogers stood over them.

"Come on," Agent Smith said, holding out his hand to help Nick up. "Rogers says she's parked illegally."

"You believe in my marriage," Toria accused. "You can't send him back—you called me Mrs. Sankovitch."

Rogers looked at her long and hard. "Unfortunately, it doesn't make a difference if I do," she said. "Rules are rules. Regulations—"

"Are regulations," Toria finished dismally.

"Sorry," Rogers said. "We'll give you some time to say goodbye. Come on, Smith."

The two agents walked away.

Toria shook her head. "Nick, I love you," she said, because there was nothing else that she could say.

"I love you, too," he said. "For always."

He kissed her, and there was still the magic—it would have to carry them through the coming miles, and years, apart.

Why did all their kisses have to be about goodbye? Toria wondered.

"Close your eyes," Nick said. "Don't watch me go."

She did as he asked, flinching only as she heard the handcuffs snapped on his wrists.

When she opened her eyes, he was gone.

SHE PARKED THE PICKUP in front of the house. The leaf-filled gutter over the front porch leaked, and Toria thought she would ask Nick to get up there on the ladder. Then she remembered he wasn't home.

Wouldn't be home for a long time.

She went to the kitchen and started to fix a cup of tea.

"I don't want this," she said. So she popped open one of Nick's sodas from the fridge.

She walked back to the living room and flipped on the television. There was a documentary on the wonders of Antarctica on public television, but she wasn't interested. *Gilligan's Island* was on Channel 8, but she started to cry when Ginger asked the professor for a date.

She sat on the bay-window cushion and watched the rain.

So unfair.

To be almost thirty, to have almost everything— husband, daughter, home, work...

Suddenly, she gasped.

A white unmarked car pull up to the path. It couldn't be, she cautioned herself, not wanting to hope and be crushed.

But she saw Agent Rogers open the passenger-side door and then Toria began laughing and crying all at the same time. She ran to the front door, then down the path, the rain soaking her face and hair.

She didn't question how long. She didn't question why.

She just threw her arms around her husband and whispered, "Welcome home."

When she pulled away to look at him, the white car floated off into the night.

"Rogers says to tell you that you have to contact the Social Security Administration to get your maiden name deleted from their records. And she also says that we need to update our income-tax records so that we'll pay the marriage penalty. And I called Missy Schroeder. She says she's taking Anya shopping tomorrow. They're getting their hair done together."

Two MONTHS LATER, Nick rolled over and snuggled spoon fashion against his wife, his hard and ready maleness pressed against her soft round hips.

"Let me understand this," he whispered. "In third grade, you were in *Indian Princesses,* but Jeanne Scherer's father had to take you and Jeanne to the September sleep-over because your dad was at a conference on linguistics in Spain. And the tent wasn't big enough for all three of you, so he slept in the rain and got pneumonia."

"Do you really think they're going to ask questions like that?" Toria purred sleepily. She closed her eyes against the light. It was too early—on the other hand, what a delicious way to wake up. Much better than an alarm clock.

"No, they're not going to ask that," Nick admitted. "But I still like to know these things. I like to know everything about you."

He turned her over, lightly caressing the soft flesh of her stomach.

"Maybe they'll ask me which breast is more responsive to me, or where you have that cute little mole or where I can touch you that makes you..."

"Nick!" she shouted in mock outrage.

He stared at her innocently.

"I just wanted to find that spot again," he said.

She arched her neck in delight. "Well, all right, but only if you're doing this for informational purposes only."

"Research," Nick said. "We call it research. But, darling, I'm not going to tell."

After Rogers relented, her superefficient and cynical heart touched by the events at the Byleukrainian restaurant, the Sankovitches had been given a second chance. Rogers had pulled every string in Washington, had called in every favor owed to her in her many years at INS, had done whatever bureaucrats do to get their way.

The Sankovitches had another interview scheduled.

A formality, really. There wasn't anybody in the country who hadn't been captivated by the story of the Sankovitch romance—though Nick and Toria refused every "media opportunity" that came to them.

"So, am I getting warm?" Nick whispered, slipping his hands between her legs.

"Very," Toria confirmed. One of the best things about Nick was that he could bring her to the brink of ecstasy in moments—or he could take his time and edge her body toward orgasm over lingering hours.

A slight gust rustled the lace curtains. From Anya's room, the music box started its waltz. Toria had given Anya the music box as a present the day after they had returned to being a family.

Nick leaned up on one elbow. "How does that music box do that?" he asked.

"It just does that sometimes," Toria said dreamily.

"She loves that thing," Nick said, sounding baffled by the attraction.

He kissed her abdomen and then looked up at her. "You have something to tell me, don't you?" he asked.

Toria felt a blush burst on her face. "What...what do you mean?"

"Your stomach, so round and at its center, so hard," Nick said. "In Byleukrainia, the at-home pregnancy test was a husband's kiss on his bride's stomach. You're having a baby."

Toria nodded shyly. "It happened the night you came home to me for good. But I thought I'd wait to tell you when I got it confirmed by the doctor."

"No need," he said, kissing her again in the warm, hard place where their baby would grow. "Byleukrainian husbands are the best pregnancy testers in the world."

He squeezed her tightly.

"I am the luckiest man alive!" he shouted, and then he abruptly rolled off her. "Did I hurt you? Was my weight too heavy? Are you all right?"

"Now, don't start that stuff," Toria warned. "Just because I'm pregnant doesn't mean I'm going to break into a million pieces... I'm not like the woman on Anya's music box."

"You're sure?"

She shoved her hand into the rich dark hair that spilled over his forehead and pulled him to her. She kissed him hungrily on the mouth.

I'm not that woman anymore, she thought, *I'm not a delicate china doll, frozen in time, waiting for my gentleman, waiting for the music to play. I've found my life.*

"Want to get married again?" Nick asked. "Can you promise to love, honor and cherish?"

"I do. What about you?"

"I do with all my heart," he said, pulling her on top of him. "I marry you now and again and again. To be honest, the first time, that was for Anya. And this time will be for love."

We hope you fell in love with
Tarini Schaskylavitch, who helped Nick and
Toria find happiness in American Romance's
MARRYING NICKY by Vivian Leiber, as
much as we did. Now you can catch Tarini in
her own book—HIS KIND OF TROUBLE also
by Vivian Leiber—coming to you
from Harlequin Intrigue
in early 1997.

Here's a sneak preview:

His Kind of Trouble

Tarini leapt for her black bag, spinning on her heels and tearing for the front door, toppling the dining room chairs in her wake.

Splattering gunfire like a violent rain across her kitchen walls, they were gaining, and they wanted her.

Badly.

She flung open the front door, ran down the stairs three at a time, jamming her hand in her purse for her gun as she ran. Like a set of keys that always landed at the bottom of the pile of junk, her gun eluded her. Bullets tagged the wall scant inches from her head. Shell casings clattered at her feet.

The lobby. If she could just get past the lobby. She could escape to the cover of darkest night—maybe even get that gun out of her purse.

Enclosed in glass, the tiny lobby had just enough room for a pile of junk mail, a withered fern and a folded baby carriage. She shoved open the security door to the lobby and tripped over a toy fire engine. Straight into the arms of a killer.

She screamed.

She didn't even have a gun in her hand, didn't have a knife, didn't even have a set of keys to jab at his face. Still, with her arms pinned, she kicked his kneecaps as hard as she could, tried to whack him with her purse, and kept hollering, hoping one of her neighbors had sense enough to call the police.

"Tarini, damn it, stop it! You're going to break my leg."

She jerked her head back.

"Austin!"

Before she could tell Austin Smith to go to hell, the glass security door behind them shattered into a thousand little carats that skittered across the floor.

"Come on!" he shouted, grabbing her hand.

They ran out into the deserted street, past a row of parked cars to his familiar red convertible Porsche. He picked her up and dumped her gracelessly into the passenger bucket seat, leaping over her head to the driver's side.

With a quick kick to the accelerator, they peeled out onto the road. Her purse landed on the floor at her feet. Her datebook, a tube of lipstick, a paperback and the gun fell out.

Finally, the gun.

Tarini had just about decided she'd left it on the nightstand.

She scooped up the Walther, thanked her lucky stars that it was loaded and looked back. Her attackers fanned out onto the road, but scattered at the approach of sirens. She didn't have a clear shot, and besides, she had made it out alive.

Austin cornered, hard, nearly hitting a car parallel parked on the left-hand side of the road. He drove on the deserted street and then turned down an alley toward a brightly lit thoroughfare.

Tarini started to breathe easier—she was alive!— then realized she had only traded a frying pan for real fire.

"You can drop me off at the corner." No way she was dying in a car wreck after surviving those goons at the apartment. If she had to, she'd jump out at the first light.

"Not so fast," Austin said. "They're hot on your heels and I'm the only guy volunteering for the job of knight in shining armor."

She rolled her eyes dramatically while inside she cringed.

He was cocky, he was arrogant, he was so damned sure of himself. But the horrible truth of the matter was he had every right to be. He was chiseled like a marble god, had the surefooted masculine charm of a mega movie star, and was smarter than any man she had ever known.

And he had just saved her life.

She had considered herself the lucky one when they had been together. She could barely contain herself, wanting to tell the whole world that she was his woman.

None of that was anything she wanted to remember now.

It was over. History. Now it was time to move on.

"Drop me off here," she insisted.

"No way am I dropping you off," he said.

"Listen, thanks for getting me out of there, but I'll just take it from here, if you don't mind."

"Don't you want to know what those guys wanted from you?"

She hadn't had any time to think in the past five minutes.

"I assume the secret police wanted to kill me because of Vladimir," she said.

"You should be so lucky. You've got something Karinolov wants," he said, pulling to a stop at the light. The light turned green, but he put on his emergency lights and cars pulled around them.

Tarini knew now would be a good time to bolt, but she was curious.

"They want my grandma's secret recipe for klatschkes?" she quipped, affecting nonchalant interest that she didn't feel.

"No," Austin said through gritted teeth. "They want Vladimir's child... The child you are carrying."

It took every ounce of her willpower not to dissolve under his narrow-eyed gaze. He hated her—God, how he hated her! He always showed his emotions in his eyes and where once there had been love, it was gone. He hated her and he had every right to. She had been the one to crisply and coolly dismiss him, refusing his phone calls and returning his letters unopened.

She had counted on him being a gentleman—the kind that didn't embarrass a lady by asking her too many questions. And he had been a gentleman when she and Vladimir told Austin of their engagement scant days after she left him, his bed—he hadn't said more than a carefully crafted congratulations.

He had never asked her to explain. Good thing.

But now there would be even more trouble because the splintering Byleukrainian government thought she was carrying the next heir to the throne.

* * * * *

DON'T MISS IT!
HIS KIND OF TROUBLE
by Vivian Leiber
Harlequin Intrigue
early 1997

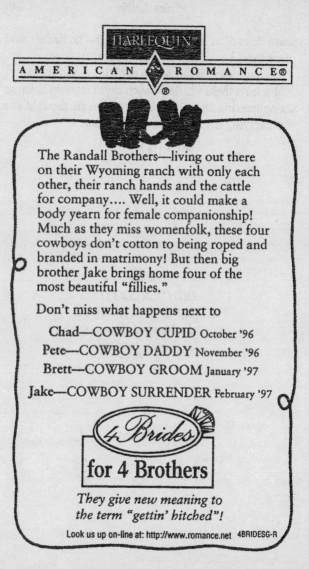

HARLEQUIN
AMERICAN ✦ ROMANCE®

The Randall Brothers—living out there on their Wyoming ranch with only each other, their ranch hands and the cattle for company.... Well, it could make a body yearn for female companionship! Much as they miss womenfolk, these four cowboys don't cotton to being roped and branded in matrimony! But then big brother Jake brings home four of the most beautiful "fillies."

Don't miss what happens next to

Chad—COWBOY CUPID October '96

Pete—COWBOY DADDY November '96

Brett—COWBOY GROOM January '97

Jake—COWBOY SURRENDER February '97

4 Brides
for 4 Brothers

They give new meaning to the term "gettin' hitched"!

1997
Reader's Engagement Book
A calendar of important dates
and anniversaries for readers to use!

Informative and entertaining—with notable
dates and trivia highlighted throughout the year.

Handy, convenient, pocketbook size to help you
keep track of your own personal important dates.

Added bonus—contains $5.00 worth of coupons
for upcoming Harlequin and Silhouette books.
This calendar more than pays for itself!

Available beginning in November at
your favorite retail outlet.

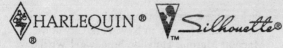

HARLEQUIN ®   Silhouette®

The collection of the year!
NEW YORK TIMES BESTSELLING AUTHORS

Linda Lael Miller
Wild About Harry

Janet Dailey
Sweet Promise

Elizabeth Lowell
Reckless Love

Penny Jordan
Love's Choices

and featuring
Nora Roberts
The Calhoun Women

This special trade-size edition features four of the wildly popular titles in the Calhoun miniseries together in one volume—a true collector's item!

Pick up these great authors and a chance to win a weekend for two in New York City at the Marriott Marquis Hotel on Broadway! We'll pay for your flight, your hotel—even a Broadway show!

Available in December at your favorite retail outlet.

NEW YORK

Marriott ®

MARQUIS

◆ HARLEQUIN® ♥ *Silhouette*®

NYT1296-R

Merry Christmas, Baby!

A romantic collection filled with the magic
of Christmas and the joy of children.

SUSAN WIGGS, Karen Young and
Bobby Hutchinson bring you Christmas wishes,
weddings and romance, in a charming
trio of stories that will warm up your
holiday season.

MERRY CHRISTMAS, BABY! also contains
Harlequin's special gift to you—a set of
FREE GIFT TAGS included in every book.

Brighten up your holiday season with
MERRY CHRISTMAS, BABY!

Available in November at
your favorite retail store.

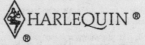

HARLEQUIN®

Don't miss these Harlequin favorites by some of our most distinguished authors! And now you can receive a discount by ordering two or more titles!

HT#25657	PASSION AND SCANDAL by Candace Schuler	$3.25 U.S. $3.75 CAN.	☐ ☐
HP#11787	TO HAVE AND TO HOLD by Sally Wentworth	$3.25 U.S. $3.75 CAN.	☐ ☐
HR#03385	THE SISTER SECRET by Jessica Steele	$2.99 U.S. $3.50 CAN	☐ ☐
HS#70634	CRY UNCLE by Judith Arnold	$3.75 U.S. $4.25 CAN.	☐ ☐
HI#22346	THE DESPERADO by Patricia Rosemoor	$3.50 U.S. $3.99 CAN	☐ ☐
HAR#16610	MERRY CHRISTMAS, MOMMY by Muriel Jensen	$3.50 U.S. $3.99 CAN.	☐ ☐
HH#28895	THE WELSHMAN'S WAY by Margaret Moore	$4.50 U.S. $4.99 CAN.	☐ ☐

(limited quantities available on certain titles)

AMOUNT	$
DEDUCT: 10% DISCOUNT FOR 2+ BOOKS	$
POSTAGE & HANDLING ($1.00 for one book, 50¢ for each additional)	$
APPLICABLE TAXES*	$_____
TOTAL PAYABLE	$_____

(check or money order—please do not send cash)

To order, complete this form and send it, along with a check or money order for the total above, payable to Harlequin Books, to: **In the U.S.:** 3010 Walden Avenue, P.O. Box 9047, Buffalo, NY 14269-9047; **In Canada:** P.O. Box 613, Fort Erie, Ontario, L2A 5X3.

Name: _____

Address: _____ City: _____

State/Prov.: _____ Zip/Postal Code: _____

*New York residents remit applicable sales taxes.
 Canadian residents remit applicable GST and provincial taxes.   HBACK-OD3

Look us up on-line at: http://www.romance.net